He'd wanted to kiss her.

Thank God he hadn't.

She would be here for four more days, and the last thing he wanted was to complicate things.

Before that moment occurred, he had just wanted to hold Ella's hands, wipe her tears. But when she had opened her eyes, he had caught a glimpse of her Sardinian sensitivity and strength...and he had been overcome with a desire to immerse himself in those depths. The first time he had felt any such desire for so long...

Massimo tossed his shirt on a chair and strode to his balcony. Looking up through his telescope at the stars or moon always relaxed him. Tonight the moon was especially luminous, and he watched it for several minutes. The night breeze was cool, but he welcomed its feathery strokes over his heated body. As he looked over the moonlit crowns of the oleander trees in the distance to the only room of the guesthouse that was lit, and where Ella would be getting ready for bed, Massimo's heart clanged with a sudden realization.

He was alive.

Dear Reader,

It makes me happy to hear that someone has found happiness, joy and love after experiencing loss. I wanted to create a story with this premise, giving my hero and heroine the opportunity to seize the moment and accept the chance the universe is offering.

My heroine, Ella Ross, has lost her adoptive parents, and my hero Massimo DiLuca's wife passed suddenly three years earlier. When Ella is offered an assignment to interview the reclusive billionaire Baron DiLuca and his mother in Sardinia for a piece in *Living the Life* magazine, Ella sees it as a chance to return to the island where she was born and to reconnect with a relative she hasn't seen since she was four. And maybe discover why her birth mother gave her up for adoption...

As Ella and Massimo spend time together discovering nuggets of each other's past, their mutual empathy and attraction, along with the enchanting Sardinian backdrop, create the alchemy for a glittering happy-ever-after.

Wishing you happiness, hope and healing (if needed), and hugs,

Rosanna xo

Falling for the Sardinian Baron

Rosanna Battigelli

ISBN-13: 978-1-335-40674-3

Falling for the Sardinian Baron

Copyright © 2021 by Rosanna Battigelli

All rights reserved. No part of this book may be used or reproduced in any manner whatsoever without written permission except in the case of brief quotations embodied in critical articles and reviews.

This is a work of fiction. Names, characters, places and incidents are either the product of the author's imagination or are used fictitiously. Any resemblance to actual persons, living or dead, businesses, companies, events or locales is entirely coincidental.

This edition published by arrangement with Harlequin Books S.A.

For questions and comments about the quality of this book, please contact us at CustomerService@Harlequin.com.

Harlequin Enterprises ULC
22 Adelaide St. West, 40th Floor
Toronto, Ontario M5H 4E3, Canada
www.Harlequin.com

Printed in U.S.A.

Rosanna Battigelli loved Harlequin Romance novels as a teenager and dreamed of being a romance writer. For a family trip to Italy when she was fifteen, she packed enough Harlequins to last the month! Rosanna's passion for reading and love of children resulted in a stellar teaching career with four Best Practice Awards. And she also pursued another passion—writing—and has been published in over a dozen anthologies. Since she's retired, her dream of being a Harlequin Romance writer has come true!

Books by Rosanna Battigelli

Harlequin Romance

Swept Away by the Enigmatic Tycoon
Captivated by Her Italian Boss
Caribbean Escape with the Tycoon
Rescued by the Guarded Tycoon

Visit the Author Profile page at Harlequin.com.

For Sarah, Jordan and Nathan, with love always.
xoxoxo

Praise for
Rosanna Battigelli

CHAPTER ONE

DESPITE THE AIR-CONDITIONING in the baggage claim area of Cagliari Airport, Ella could feel the prickling sensation of perspiration beading along her temples. She took off her jean jacket and stuffed it into her carry-on luggage before rifling through her handbag for an elastic band to put up her hair in a ponytail.

Watching the last of the passengers retrieve their luggage from the conveyor belt and head for the exits, she wondered at the cause of her driver's delay. Gregoriu Pinna was to have been at the airport early, waiting for her.

Flinging her handbag over one shoulder, Ella propped her small carry-on on top of her larger suitcase and turned around swiftly, her luggage ramming hard into a body.

She gasped at the same time that her victim expelled a loud grunt, the force of the impact making him lose his footing momentarily, but he managed not to fall. Ella let her hand drop from covering her mouth. *"Mi scusi,"* she apologized, squinting up at him as she retrieved her carry-on. "I didn't see you..." And then she realized she had slipped into English. *"Non—"*

"I understand English" came the man's clipped reply.

Ella's mouth snapped shut, and she waited, expecting him to respond with a gracious "No worries." But he just stood there, his sunglasses and thick beard most likely concealing an irritated expression that mirrored the edge in his voice. He wore a navy T-shirt that revealed tanned, muscled arms, and faded jeans, from what she could make out in the two-second shift of her gaze.

"You are Ella Ross." His tone was dry, and his lips had twisted slightly.

"Um, yes," she said, frowning. "But you're not—"

"—Gregoriu Pinna."

She arched an eyebrow. "So you're taking his place? Is he okay? I was worried that he might have been in an accident..."

"He was not."

Ella let out a sigh of relief. She waited for the man to say more. Explain what had happened to make *him* take Gregoriu's place. But he just stood there, appraising her coolly. She felt her cheeks tingling with what she knew would immediately be a telltale flush.

Did she have to pull every word out of this guy's mouth? And why was he dressed in such casual clothes? Where were his navy jacket and trousers? The gold D embroidered on the jacket's lapel, she had been informed, would be the way to identify a DiLuca employee.

Ella's boss at *Living the Life* magazine had been contacted by an agent of reclusive Sardinian billionaire Massimo DiLuca to have the DiLuca family interviewed for the lead story in August. Publisher and editor-in-chief, Paul Ramsay, had offered *her* the assignment.

She shifted as a wave of fatigue hit her. Was he intending to stand there indefinitely? She was starting to get a kink in her neck, looking up at this skyscraper of a man.

And then the thought occurred to her that maybe this emissary's English was limited. She felt a twinge of remorse for being so judgmental.

"And *you* are…?" she said in as polite a tone as she could muster.

"Gregoriu's replacement." He reached for her luggage. "Follow me, please. I will take you to the hotel." He turned and started walking toward the exit.

Ella hesitated. He had a strong Italian accent

but seemed able to communicate well enough. Could this guy be an imposter? Perhaps he had done something terrible to Gregoriu after squeezing some information out of the poor guy, and now he was pretending to be someone he was not. Maybe he was looking to rob her after driving to some secluded spot. She glanced around worriedly, trying to spot a security officer.

The man swiveled around suddenly, and Ella remained where she was, blinking up at him for a few seconds before finally blurting, "*Scusi*, but I think you should show me your ID."

Is that a flash of a smile? Ella wondered. *Or just a shadow?*

He released his hold on the luggage, reached into the back pocket of his jeans and pulled out his wallet. He strode over to her and flipped it open.

Ella peered at the photo. No sunglasses, no cap. Dark hair and a groomed scruff, not a thick beard. Noticeably long eyelashes that framed dark, almond-shaped eyes that looked rimmed with eyeliner. Her pulse quickened. She recognized the face on the photo. She had seen it during her research, and it had always appeared above a designer suit. She hadn't found anything more recent than three years earlier. Ella's gaze flew to the information identifying him, but she didn't have to. She just needed a few moments to collect herself and try to stop the flush on her cheeks from becoming an intense flame.

As calmly as she could, Ella gazed up at Baron Massimo DiLuca.

"Grazie, signor barone DiLuca," she said, nodding, her voice as clipped as the stiletto heels walking past them. Massimo almost chuckled at the formality of her tone. He might be a baron and one of the richest men in Sardinia, if not Italy, but he certainly did not need to be addressed in such a stiff and formal manner.

"My title is not necessary, *signorina* Ross," he told her drily. "I'm fine with just *signor*. Actually, given the fact that we're about to spend a week under the same roof, *Massimo* is even better."

Her brows arched but she didn't reply.

"And I suppose I should apologize, not introducing myself right away." He looked around. "I just didn't want anyone to hear me… People make a big fuss when they find out I'm around. And then the cell phones come out to snap a thousand pictures, and the inevitable reporter appears and starts hounding me." He gestured toward the exit. "*Andiamo.* Let's go." He shoved his leather wallet back into his jeans pocket and wheeled Ella's luggage ahead of him. When he came to the revolving doors, he stopped and gestured for her to precede him.

Moments later, Massimo had placed her suitcase and carry-on in the trunk of his silver-gray SUV and Ella was sitting in the passenger seat next to him, her handbag in her lap. While she was absorbed in putting on her seat belt, his gaze took in her travel-tousled hair in its ponytail—light brown with what looked like natural gold highlights—her slender neck and arms, and a loose-fitting coral cotton dress that had bunched up when she sat down, revealing smooth, shapely legs. She had applied coral nail polish on her fingernails and the same to her toenails, which peeked out of low-heeled wedge sandals.

Massimo looked away before she could catch him staring. The last thing he wanted was to make her uncomfortable and to give her the wrong impression of him.

It was just that this Ella Ross was younger than he'd expected. In his early communication with her boss, Massimo had requested someone who was proficient in Italian and good—no, *excellent*—at his or her job. That was one of his expected criteria of anyone in his employ. If they valued their job, they would strive for and achieve excellence, he reasoned. This belief extended from those who worked at his luxury resorts to his housekeepers and personal chef.

Massimo had conveyed to him that he wanted an experienced journalist who would demonstrate cultural sensitivity toward his family, especially since his mother's English was limited.

The woman now sitting next to Massimo was the right person for the assignment, her boss had claimed, and had proceeded to sing her praises. Massimo had followed up with his own online search. The first article he found was from the *New York Times* and included a photo of Ella Ross accepting an award. It was a side shot, so he had been able to see only her profile, partially obscured by her shoulder-length brown hair and dark-framed glasses. She was wearing a navy business suit and low-heeled shoes. The article had mentioned that Ella Ross had won some prestigious news-paper-and-magazine award for excellence in journalism.

That had satisfied him that her boss had made the right choice. And it had pleased his mother when he had told her.

But seeing her up close at the airport, in

a ponytail and casual cotton dress, Ella had looked barely older than twenty-one, if that. And it had taken him aback, although he had no intention of showing it.

Massimo realized he was tapping the side of the steering wheel. He glanced back at Ella, nodded and started the ignition. Once he had left the airport parking lot and had merged into the Cagliari traffic, he said, "I suppose you are hungry, no? Before we head to the hotel, I will stop at a *pasticceria*. You can have a snack... perhaps a brioche or one of our traditional Sardinian pastries. I could use an espresso, too..."

"It's not necessary, but if you need to stop for a caffeine fix—" she gave a soft laugh "—I'm game." And then, as if embarrassed by the familiarity of her tone, her smile dissipated and she shifted her gaze to the rows of pastel-colored buildings and clusters of tourists and locals ready for post-siesta shopping.

He frowned. His English was quite good, but there were phrases now and then that were baffling. What *game* was she wanting or expecting to play? He pursed his lips. Perhaps he should test *her* proficiency of Italian. He certainly didn't expect her to know or understand any of the Sardinian dialect, which was very different from the official Italian language.

"Che tipo di caffè prende? O preferisce una bevanda fresca?"

She turned to him with raised brows. *"Un espresso va benissimo. Oppure una limonata."* She shrugged and gave a small laugh, a sound that reminded Massimo of one of the delicate chimes in his island garden. "I suppose it all depends on how hot I am when we enter the pastry shop."

Hearing her speak Italian perfectly sent an unexpected tingle through Massimo's veins. There was no awkward pausing or butchering of the pronunciation. Her words had flowed out quickly and smoothly, without hesitation. If he didn't know any better, he'd think Ella Ross was Italian.

Massimo nodded, and concentrating on the winding road ahead, he thought about the word *hot*. She had used it innocently, of course, but he couldn't help thinking about its other meaning, a meaning that he was perfectly aware of…and how it applied to his guest.

He shook his head. He shouldn't even be having such thoughts. It didn't matter to him whether Ella Ross was *hot* or not. She wasn't here to bewitch him with her fawn-like eyes, perfect coral lips and curvy body. She was here to do one thing and one thing only: interview him and his mother for next month's lead story in *Living the Life*.

"Oh, look, a wedding!"

His passenger's enthused tone jolted him out of his thoughts. Massimo slowed down to a stop behind a line of cars that had done the same to catch a glimpse of the activity in front of the medieval high-domed Cathedral of Santa Maria. The bride and groom were holding hands and posing for the photographer while the group around them watched. Elaborate flower arrangements in huge ceramic planters were positioned on either side of the massive, engraved double wooden doors and down the stairs to the road, their fuchsia blooms matching the gowns of the bridesmaids' dresses and the bride's bouquet.

"Aw…" Ella said as the groom kissed his bride and suddenly swept her off her feet to twirl her around. The crowd erupted in cheers, and moments later, the photographer gave the signal for the tossing of the confetti.

Massimo felt a tightening in his chest. The scene had ignited memories that still felt like arrows piercing his heart. He and his wife had gotten married at this cathedral, and watching the young couple in front of the ornate facade now was like having his past flash in front of him.

He felt another jolt at the applause and cries

of *"Bravo, bravo"* as the groom gave his bride a second and more thorough kiss.

Ella turned to him sheepishly, her cheeks flushed. "I'm a sucker for rom—um—I mean happy events…" Her words trailed off, and her smile disappeared as she met his gaze.

He caught his own expression in the rear-view mirror. His brows were furrowed, his lips compressed in a hard line. No wonder she was looking at him strangely.

The car in front of him started moving and Massimo focused his attention on driving, aware of the Vespa riders that were zooming in and out of traffic, taking every opportunity to get ahead.

He turned into a side road, and a couple of minutes later, pulled into a parking lot that was almost full. *"Ecco. Siamo arrivati!"* He leaped out of the SUV and opened the door for his guest. *"Prego."* He nodded, gesturing for her to step out. "We are here at the *Pasticceria della Mamma*. Now you can get your espresso or lemonade."

He couldn't help glimpsing the length of her legs as she swung around and got out. A sudden seaside breeze made her dress billow up, and a couple of young men across the street gave a low whistle. He scowled at them, and they laughed and walked away.

"Not all tourists show good manners," he said curtly as they entered the pastry shop. "Or control." He led her to an empty table in the back corner of the room, one of a dozen that were painted the same colors as the macarons in the glass display that ran the length of the counter.

He removed his sunglasses and smiled at the approaching waitress before looking expectantly at Ella.

"Un espresso, grazie." She smiled at the waitress and glanced at the display of pastries. "Oh, my goodness, I can't resist," she said with a laugh. *"Una sebada, per favore."*

Massimo's brows arched. She had obviously done some research, requesting a traditional Sardinian dessert—a sweet pastry that was fried and filled with lemon-scented pecorino and topped with warm honey.

"Lo stesso per me, Maria," he said, flashing a smile at the waitress.

"You didn't have to tell me, *signor* DiLuca," she replied cheerfully with a heavy Italian accent. "You order that nine times out of ten!"

He laughed and caught Ella's gaze on him. She really did have fawn eyes, dark and wide—like the expanse of sea he'd often look out at from his bedroom balcony at midnight— Whoa! Why was his mind even formulating such thoughts? She was here on business, and he had no business conjuring up thoughts like that about her. Thoughts that sounded like they were part of a romantic sonnet...

He was not interested in romance.

Been there, done that.

And it had left him with a broken heart.

CHAPTER TWO

ELLA'S GAZE WENT from the baron's eyes to the dimple in his cheek. He was so distractingly good-looking... And although she generally wasn't a huge fan of beards, his was rather attractive. Thick but tapered in all the right spots, his sideburns descending evenly to his jaw, his moustache perfectly symmetrical. And below his lips—completely visible and perfectly shaped—the inverted triangle of hair above his beard made him look like what she imagined a baron would look like, even though his baseball cap, T-shirt and jeans made him appear an ordinary guy...if you could call strong, tanned biceps, broad shoulders and a muscled chest ordinary.

God, she was *staring*! Ella averted her gaze as the waitress arrived with their espressos and *sebadas*. As she sipped her espresso, her thoughts flew to her previous boyfriends. There were two guys she had dated at university for a while—a short while—but she had been too focused on her studies to even consider letting things develop beyond a certain point. Both had wanted more than she was willing to give, and Ella had been the one each time to end the relationship.

Her last boyfriend had been a writer named Dustin whom she had met a couple of years after starting her current job.

As a freelancer, he had contributed to *Living the Life* magazine. Since he lived in Toronto, Ella's boss had shared the connection. Dustin had been the one to contact her, first by email and then by phone. Ella had liked his easy manner and sense of humor, and after a few phone conversations, he had asked her out. They had done dinner, the movies, a basketball game, and he had even taken her for dinner at his parents' home.

He was good-looking, with dirty-blond hair and blue eyes. They had spent about a month getting together for dinners, shows and the occasional stroll in scenic High Park. They had kissed after about a week of dating, but his kisses hadn't stirred her. Hadn't activated her pulse.

Ella had been comfortable with him, but she had never felt the desire, the electricity—not even a spark—that the heroines in the novels she read seemed to experience.

She had wondered at her lack of desire, let alone passion, and the thought occurred to her that maybe she was putting all her ardor into her career. She loved traveling, interviewing people around the world and working on her pieces for her magazine in her upscale Toronto condo overlooking High Park. Maybe she just didn't want to give up her independence... As the weeks had gone by, Ella had realized she liked Dustin more as a friend and colleague than as a date, and she had decided it wasn't fair to let him think there was a future for them together.

After the dinner at his parents' place, it became clear to Ella that Dustin thought things were just fine between them and introducing her to his family indicated his more serious intentions. It had jolted her, and she knew she had to make him aware that they were not on the same page and they should stop dating. He had been hurt—and she had felt bad about it—but ultimately, it had been the kindest thing to do.

He had sent her an email a couple of months later, saying he had connected with someone he was certain was his soulmate and he hoped he and Ella could remain on friendly terms.

And they had, occasionally emailing or chatting on the phone.

Ella thought about what her adoptive mother had told her when she had confided in her about Dustin and guys in general. "If he doesn't put stars in your eyes, then he's not the right one for *you*."

This memory made Ella's heart ache. She missed her mom, and the tight relationship they had shared, which some of her friends had envied. She had been able to talk to her about anything, and Cassandra had listened, encouraged, advised, comforted and cheered Ella on. Every daughter should be so lucky…

She remembered how one of her classmates had once blurted, "And she's not even your real mom," after overhearing Ella say in a conversation she was adopted, and Ella had turned to her, her eyes glinting ice. "She is my real mom," she had replied in staccato tones, and the girl had smirked and walked off. Later, Ella had shared her hurt feelings with her mother, who had drawn her into her arms and murmured, "If I'm not real, then who was it that made your favorite Sardinian dessert for you tonight?"

Ella couldn't help smiling, her memories of her mother now bringing her more smiles than tears, unlike the first year after her mom had passed. As Ella bit into the pastry she had loved since childhood, she closed her eyes and nodded. "Heavenly," she said with a contented sigh. "I'll have to start making them again…" Her last word trailed off, and she groaned inwardly. She really had to think before blabbing away. She wasn't here to tell the baron anything about herself or her connection to Sardinia.

"You've made these before?" Massimo's eyes narrowed as they peered at her over his espresso cup.

"Um, yeah, I went through a 'let's cook something from around the world' phase," she fibbed. "I was intrigued by what I read about Sardinia, cooking or otherwise…although I didn't have fresh pecorino, so I used ricotta instead." She bit into her *sebada* again, savoring the lemon-scented pecorino mingling with the honey. "Man, this is really good. Do you cook? Or bake? Oh, how silly," she said with a chuckle. "Of course a baron wouldn't be doing his own cooking. Or his wi—"

She stopped in horror. She had been making a general statement but realized how inappropriate it was—especially the last part—since the baron had lost his wife three years earlier. She had read about it online while doing her research. It had saddened her, and the accompanying photo of the two of them on their wedding day had jolted her, left her wondering if she would ever look at a man adoringly the way the baron's wife was gazing at him.

Now she bit her lip hard, mortified at her insensitivity and impulsiveness. The baron's mouth had compressed into a thin line, and his forehead had creased momentarily. Ella's heart sank. He had caught her gaffe. Her mind scrambled for the right words to apologize...

Massimo drank his espresso and set down his demitasse. When his gaze returned to her, his mouth had curved into a smile. And there was a glint of amusement in his dark eyes. And no sign of a frown. Perhaps he hadn't caught the near *wife* reference after all... *Thank God*.

"Actually, being a *human*, I enjoy cooking. Mind you, I do have a chef, also, but there are days when I'm in the mood to be alone and, how do you say, whip up my own dinner. Try something new..."

Ella nodded. "I like to try new dishes, too," she said, breathing an inward sigh of relief.

"Another espresso?" he asked, as the waitress brought him a second cup.

"No, *grazie*. I'm good. And good to go." She unclasped her handbag and reached inside for her wallet.

"*Per carità*... You are my guest. The bill is

taken care of." Massimo's voice brooked no argument, and she looked up and met his enigmatic gaze.

He downed his espresso before rising to stand behind her, a hand on her chair.

She stood up, and he tucked her chair in as she moved aside, his arm brushing against hers for a moment. She caught her breath involuntarily and, hoping that the tingle in her cheeks wouldn't change to a traitorous flush, she strode brusquely to the door.

"*Signor* DiLuca, if I may ask," she ventured as they buckled up moments later, "you didn't seem to be worried about people coming up to you in the pastry shop."

"Please... Massimo." His eyes pierced hers. "That's because the *Pasticceria della Mamma* is where the tourists go. And they don't know who I am. The locals go elsewhere." He put on his sunglasses, engaged the clutch, and seconds later, he was pressing the accelerator. He shot her a glance. "And now to the hotel..."

"Is it very far?"

"About twenty-five minutes from here... But don't worry. You don't need to make conversation. You'll be too busy looking at the view."

"I'm not worried," she replied lightly. "And I don't generally have a problem making conversation."

"Of course not. That's your job."

After leaving the congested street of the cathedral, Massimo stepped on the accelerator, and in a few moments, they were on the highway heading south.

The Baron was right; who wanted to talk with a view like this? The bewitching sun-sparkled sea with its varying shades of turquoise, blue green, cerulean, blending into and over each other, and far off in the distance, deepening to royal blue and even indigo. Sailboats bobbing on gentle waves. A cloudless baby-blue sky that looked like a perfectly pressed bedsheet…

There were bursts of color at every turn. Magenta bougainvillea trailing over terraces and balconies, poppies gently waving their brilliant red-orange faces at them as Massimo drove by, plush-looking hills and mountain sides streaked with golden broom.

The coastal route was breathtaking with its adjacent sandy beach that looked like a long strip of sifted white flour. Limestone crags and unusual rocky formations leaned into the sea, and Ella was sure that she spotted ancient granite caves like the ones she had read about in her travel guides about Sardinia, opened by the Romans who had conquered the island. As they passed a secluded cove, Ella exclaimed at the sight of a colony of pink flamingos.

Massimo slowed down and veered off to the shoulder of the road so she could take some photos. "Our beautiful island is on the route of many migrating birds," he told her. "You will see many other wonders while you are here…"

Massimo opened the sunroof window and a salt-tinged breeze wafted through the vehicle, diffusing the musky scent of Massimo's cologne, mingling it with hers. Ella breathed in and out slowly. This was her first visit to Sardinia since she was four, and now she could kick herself for not having booked a trip earlier, like after she had graduated.

But then again, she really hadn't had the time. She had won a national writing contest in one of the leading Canadian newspapers, subsequently getting a part-time job there doing lifestyle pieces, and then worked her way up to doing court reporting and city-beat articles. Eventually she had applied for a position at *Living the Life* magazine. Her pieces in the national paper had impressed the owner of *Living the Life*, and he had hired her. Paul Ramsay's magazine was distributed all over the world and featured extravagant and sometimes elusive celebrities and VIPs. The magazine would cover all her travel expenses when Ella needed to interview someone face-to-face.

"Some celebrities and personalities are demanding that way," Paul had said with a smile in a follow-up meeting online. "I'm sure you won't mind…"

And she hadn't. She had traveled to California, Vancouver, Paris, Rome, Ireland, the Caribbean, and of course, New York. How could she have turned down the assignment and the opportunity to spend the first week in July at Massimo DiLuca's exclusive private island off Sardinia?

And now here she was, on the island where she was born…and had been given up for adoption…

A wave of emotion swept through her and she felt a prickle at the corners of her eyes. Where would she be now if her biological mother hadn't given her up? What would she be doing? She turned her head to dab at her eyes before any tears could emerge. Since Paul had offered her this assignment two weeks ago, her mind had been a whirlwind, thinking not only about the interview but also about the emotional impact going back to Sardinia would have on her.

Ella had thought about her family history, which her boss knew nothing about, and how returning to the place of her birth was something she had considered, especially in the last couple of years...

The universe was providing her with the chance to reconnect with her adoptive father's family and perhaps discover what she could about the mother who had given her up twenty-eight years ago...and maybe find her...

She blinked.

"Are you okay? Did something get in your eye?" Massimo pressed the panel to close the sunroof and checked the air-conditioning.

"I'm fine," she said. "My eyes must be sensitive from lack of sleep. Usually I have no problem falling asleep on overnight flights... The wine helps," she added, forcing a light chuckle. "But for some reason, I was a little restless this time."

"Well, soon enough, you'll be at the hotel, and you can catch up on your sleep." Massimo gestured with one hand toward the glimmering expanse of sea. "The sound of the waves outside your window will be like a—a *ninna nanna*."

"A lullaby." She nodded. "I wish! I'll have to imagine it. My hotel isn't near the sea. My boss gave all the details to your employee in charge of the arrangements..."

Ella saw the corner of his mouth twitch

slightly, puzzling her. He obviously knew where he was going—Paul had sent him the details of the hotel—so how did he not know it wasn't by the sea? There was something else that perplexed her about him, and that was why *he* had replaced Gregoriu instead of one of his other employees, given his reluctance to engage with the public. Surely a baron had more important things to do? Seeing to the running of his own ancestral estate? Perhaps meeting with a high-ranking politician to discuss initiatives for the tourist industry? Making a sizeable donation to a children's charity? Ella had noticed earlier that he wasn't wearing his wedding band. Perhaps it was a painful reminder of his loss…

She couldn't help wondering if there was anyone new in his life. Nothing in her research had indicated that he was seeing anyone; perhaps there was a Sardinian custom about dating after a period of bereavement.

Ella checked her watch. She had planned to spend the day doing more research at her hotel before the DiLuca employee picked her up to bring her to the baron's private island. It would be a couple of days before the interview actually started, which was plenty of time to search out more details about this elusive tycoon. Doing the DiLuca piece was important—a publishing coup for the magazine, actually—and she wanted to make sure she hadn't missed anything that might enhance the story.

The interview and subsequent piece were her first priority. Maybe, if she wrapped up early, she'd attempt to call her uncle. But now was not the time to think about that…

She wondered if Massimo DiLuca would think she was nosy if she inquired about Gregoriu. She might as well; if it was a private matter, he would tell her. "*Scusi, signor* Massimo, I was just wondering…about Gregoriu, I just hope he's okay?"

Massimo slowed down and stopped at a traffic intersection. He turned to Ella. "I'm sure Gregoriu would be happy to know that you were concerned about him. Let me reassure you, so you don't lose sleep over it… Gregoriu had to rush his wife to the hospital."

"Oh, my goodness! Is she okay?" She frowned. "I'm so sorry to hear that."

"Don't be sorry. Gregoriu and Lia are now the proud parents of an eight-pound, two-ounce baby girl." He flashed her a smile before putting his foot back on the accelerator.

Massimo concentrated on the road as he drove along the coastline, glancing occasionally at the *americana* in the seat next to him. He should actually refer to her as *canadese,* since the former was a general term for anyone living in North America and the latter applied specifically to Canadians. She had exclaimed and clapped in pleasure at the baby news and then had fallen strangely silent, her brow knitting as she gazed out the window.

The next time he glanced her way, her eyes were closed and her head had drooped slightly in his direction. At any moment, he expected her to land against his shoulder or upper arm. The thought caused his muscles to tense.

He looked over again after concentrating on a sharp curve in the road, and Ella's head was now aiming for his chest. Her soft hair brushed against his upper arm, and he drew in his breath involuntarily. Her perfume had a fresh, zesty scent, like that of winter mandarins, and her thick eyelashes rested above cheeks that were peach pink. He swerved slightly, causing a rush of adrenalin, and he cursed under his breath over his momentary distraction. Thank goodness he had been on an isolated stretch of road, having switched off the coastal highway minutes before. And the movement, followed by the jerking of the gears caused her to move away from him and continue to nap, to his relief.

He took a few deep breaths to slow down his pulse and concentrated on driving but was unable to keep his passenger from entering his thoughts.

Like the way her eyes had widened in genuine dismay when she had almost mentioned his wife. He could tell that she hadn't meant to specifically refer to Rita. So he had pretended to be unaware...

He sighed, recalling how the moments, weeks and months after Rita's passing had been a blur. He'd lost her suddenly, the cause being a heart defect that no one in her family had been aware of. She had collapsed during a garden party at his parents' villa, where he and Rita had lived in one wing, and although the ambulance had arrived quickly, she was gone by the time it had passed through the ornate, automated enclosure to the villa.

He hadn't been able to carry on in his position as President and CEO of the family business. His mother, who had shared the helm with his father before *his* passing two years earlier, had taken over again for a couple of months, allowing Massimo time to grieve away from the public eye. Massimo had been devastated over losing his father, with whom he had shared a tight bond, and the shock of his wife's unexpected death had siphoned his will to continue working.

DiLuca Luxury Resorts was a billion-dollar industry that attracted clients with deep pockets to the many dozens of incomparable resorts nestled in Sardinia's most enchanting and picturesque bays. People came for the breathtaking views of the sea, unspoiled beaches and the unique culture of an island which had been coveted and dominated by, among others, the Phoenician, Roman, Spanish, Piedmont, and ultimately, Italian populations.

Massimo had eventually returned but had chosen to continue a large part of his responsibilities from his home office, instead of DiLuca headquarters in the capital city of Cagliari.

Massimo glanced at Ella. She had to be exhausted after her delayed flight. They'd be at the hotel in a few minutes, and she could go to bed right away if she wished. Or if she preferred, she could rest, take a refreshing shower and then dine with him in the hotel's two-Michelin-starred restaurant.

When he finally stopped at the hotel doors, Ella started, her eyelids struggling to stay open. She blinked, straightened and peered out the window at the gold lettering on the entrance doors. *Villa Paradiso.* She swiveled in her seat to face him. "This isn't my hotel, *si-*

gnor DiLuca. There must be some mistake… I had booked a night's stay at *L'Albergo al Sole.*"

Massimo raised an eyebrow. "I am aware of that. But I cannot have my guest stay at anything but a five-star resort."

"My hotel was four stars," she countered, "and I know your family is generously footing the bill, but I can't expect you to pay for something like *this*. It's much too much."

"You will like it here, you will see. I've already notified *L'Albergo al Sole.*" Massimo promptly climbed from the car and greeted the concierge.

A moment later, Ella stepped out and went around to his side. Her eyes widened at the sight of the luxury cars in the parking area, two of them his. She held up a hand in protest. "I can't expect you to—"

"*Signorina* Ross, it is only for one night. Please accept our Sardinian hospitality… My mother would be very upset at me if she found out you had stayed elsewhere. And it's very embarrassing to be scolded by your Sardinian *mamma* when you're thirty-six," he added with a smirk.

"Fine," she conceded with a sigh. "I wouldn't want to start on the wrong foot with your mother. *Grazie*. And if I can call you Massimo, you can call me Ella."

"*Prego.* Okay. Now let's go in. I'm sure you're anxious to relax in your room. As I am."

"You're…?" She frowned, cocking her head slightly.

"Staying overnight as well, and tomorrow I will take you myself to my villa. *Andiamo.* The concierge will bring up your luggage."

"I—I'll just need my carry-on, thanks."

"Va bene." He walked over to say a few words to the security guard at the door before gesturing to Ella to step ahead of him. When she got to the door, her gaze froze on the door handles, two large gold Ds.

"Is this—?"

"Yes, one of my resorts." He nodded and flashed her a smile. "Welcome to *Villa Paradiso.*"

Massimo was pleased with Ella's reaction as they strode through the marble foyer, past the intricately carved wooden table with its massive pedestal vase filled with a flamboyant arrangement of red roses and a variety of lilies.

He greeted the employees at the check-in desk, introduced Ella and shared the news about Gregoriu. After their clapping and exclamations subsided, Massimo informed them that he looked forward to dining at the restaurant in an hour or so.

Moments later, they handed him a room key, which he glanced at before passing it to Ella. "If there is anything you require, please do not hesitate to call the front desk," he told her. He gestured toward the gleaming gold elevator doors. "After you. I will show you to your room."

When the doors opened up to the seventh floor, Ella gasped at the view from the large floor-to-ceiling windows opposite them. She rushed over and placed her palms directly on the glass as she peered out at the endless stretch of sea.

"Oh, my God," she breathed. "This *is* paradise. I couldn't tell this place was built on the side of a hill. This view is…breathtaking."

"I'm glad you like it. Hopefully, you will like your room, as well."

"Are you kidding me?" Ella murmured moments later as she stepped into her suite. Massimo watched as she did a 360-degree visual sweep of it, her eyes widening as she took in the spaciousness and luxury of the appliances and furnishings. And the king-size bed, with its two-tone turquoise duvet and fluffy assorted pillows. She gave another gasp at the sight of the doors opening to a room-length balcony overlooking the sea. "I must have a peek," she told him and was gone before he could respond.

He watched as she surveyed the expanse of water, her hands gripping the balcony railing. He could hear the soft gush of the waves and knew it wouldn't be long before they would be lulling her to sleep. His gaze shifted to the king-size bed. Ella was small; she would be lost in it…

Why were his thoughts veering in that direction? In the three years he'd been living without Rita, he had never entertained the idea of dating another woman, let alone imagining one in bed. Not that he was imagining Ella and *himself* in the same bed; he had just pictured her there alone, nestled under the huge duvet…a two-second blip that meant nothing.

So why was he suddenly feeling so disloyal to Rita's memory?

He frowned. He should go. He'd like nothing more than to take a relaxing shower to ease some of the tension he had in his shoulders, have a glass of wine on *his* balcony while the sea breeze dried his hair and then go to dinner.

His suite was a floor above hers and twice the size. It was his haven when he had business to take care of in Cagliari, and when he did not, the suite was never used for other people. And although for the last year, he had spent a portion of his day communicating online instead of in person, it was always a pleasure when he was here to take in the spectacular sunrises and sunsets at the first resort built by his family.

Ella came back in, shaking her head. "I can't believe this. A terraced hillside resembling the Garden of Eden, a massive infinity pool and that gorgeous sea. Right outside my window. Am I dreaming?"

Massimo gave her a terse smile. "No, but you will be soon." He turned to leave and then stopped at the door. "Please take all the time you need tomorrow. You'll probably still have jet lag." He reached into his back pocket and pulled out a card. "Call me when you're ready to leave… Oh, here is your carry-on." He thanked the employee, and when the latter had gone, Massimo turned to face Ella again. "If you're not too tired, you are welcome to join me in the restaurant in an hour. If you are, I will wish you good-night now, Ella," he said with a curt nod. "And *sogni d'oro*."

CHAPTER THREE

ELLA WATCHED AS the baron strode out of her room, glad he couldn't see her eyes prickling at his last words. Words only one man—her father Micheli—had ever said to her.

Ella had loved her adoptive parents Cassandra and Micheli, and she could still remember the sadness in their lives when Micheli died. She had been only four years old, but she occasionally had a cloudy memory of crying in the home they were sharing with Micheli's parents.

Most of what she knew about him was from stories her mother had told her, although Ella did have vague memories of sitting on her father's lap while he read to her and of him singing her a song at bedtime with funny-sounding words before kissing her good-night and murmuring *"Sogni d'oro."*

Of course she eventually discovered from her mother that the song was a traditional

Sardinian lullaby. Ella hoped she would certainly have *sweet dreams* as her father, and now Massimo, had wished her before leaving. *Dreams of gold* was the literal translation, and it seemed so apt, especially with the sun beginning to set right now, a saffron ball in a gold-streaked sky.

Just watching the horizon change, like an artist's palette, before her eyes made her heart twinge. She had missed twenty-four years of skies like this, having been only four when her mother had moved them back to Canada. Not that she didn't love Canada; it boasted spectacular beauty from coast-to-coast, with its stunning oceans, majestic Rocky Mountains, lush valleys with world-class vineyards, and diverse landscapes and varying climates in each province.

Living in Ontario, dotted with over two hundred and fifty thousand lakes, Ella had loved exploring the rugged northern shores of Lake Superior and the picturesque places around the other Great Lakes. Her apartment was just north of Toronto, so she was close to Lake Ontario, an hour away from Lake Simcoe, and close enough to the magnificent Muskokas, with their pretty towns and smaller lakes with such fanciful names as Fairy Lake, Butterfly Lake, and Honey Harbour.

But being in the country where she was born, stepping on Sardinian soil and breathing the sea air outside just moments ago, a bevy of emotions were now swirling within her, causing a bittersweet ache in her chest.

This was still her country. She had dual citizenship, and over the years, she had wondered when she would be able to return. Her mother hadn't had the same desire, too heartbroken over the loss of Ella's father and the memories they had shared there.

When Micheli's father had died, Ella's mother had called to give her condolences and arranged for flowers to be delivered to Micheli's mother. And then when *she* had died eight months later, Ella's mother had sent the floral bouquet to Micheli's only brother, Domenicu. Ella had been nine when her *nonno* and *nonna* had passed, but she still had memories of her mother telling her about them.

Cassandra had occasionally called Domenicu after that, but over the years, the communications had dwindled. As well as the reasons to return to Sardinia. Cassandra had been working two jobs to support herself and Ella, and traveling out of country had not been possible, for reasons of time and money.

And Ella had been focused on her studies, and later, her job.

Cassandra had kept phone numbers and addresses of the relatives in a small notebook that Ella had found in her mother's kitchen drawer weeks after the funeral. Ella had tucked it away in her handbag, overwhelmed with grief, but when Paul had offered her the assignment in Sardinia, she had pulled it out, added the number to her cell phone contacts and had gone online to try to find information about her uncle.

Her heart had skipped a beat when she'd found that his number and address were the same, but Ella had had no intention of actually contacting him before her trip. She had a job to do with relatively short notice and she hadn't wanted any emotion dealing with her past to interfere with her task.

Now, finally back in Sardinia, reconnecting with her uncle was a real possibility if she still had the nerve. Ella had extended her stay by one week after her assignment, but she had begun to question if she could deal with such an emotional reunion in such a short amount of time. And the even greater emotional ramifications of finding her birth mother. Maybe she could plan a longer trip in the future and deal with everything then...

Ella forced herself to switch her thoughts to the man she would be interviewing in the coming week. Intrigued by the brief information her boss had given her, Ella had begun doing some preliminary research on the Di-Luca family, and surprisingly, there wasn't as much information as she had expected to find. It seemed that the DiLuca family of the current century had preferred to be more low-key than the past generations of barons and baronesses. Except until now, with the upcoming official opening of a state-of-the-art cardiac research center in Cagliari, which they had funded.

Massimo DiLuca and his mother had conceived of the project to honor their respective spouses, with the hope that continuing research would save future lives. They had enlisted an international team of architects and medical experts, and the complex would soon open its doors to accommodate some of the top cardiac researchers in the world. The upcoming ribbon-cutting ceremony would be followed by a seven-course dinner with musical entertainment and dancing in one of the building's international symposium halls.

In the latest media releases about the project, there had been speculation as to whether Massimo DiLuca would preside at the ceremony with his mother, since he had avoided the public spotlight for three years. Was the reclusive billionaire ready to face the world again?

Ella had found a few photos and articles about Massimo's parents and their investment into the resort business and how it had taken off. And then she had come across the shocking news that Massimo had lost his wife suddenly, three years earlier. Ella had stared at the online obituary of Rita Floris—she had kept her maiden name, like most Italian women—and the photo of Rita, smiling indirectly at someone. She had felt deep sadness for the loss of such a young life, and for her widowed husband.

She could understand why the baron would want to stay out of the limelight while dealing with his grief. And she doubted even now, after three years, he would bring up anything personal about himself or his late wife during the interview.

A shiver ran through her at the recollection of her first glimpse of the baron, with his strong chest and arms in a muscle-revealing T-shirt and jeans, and his abrupt, elusive manner that had made her imagination go wild. Ella shook her head, wanting to erase the memory of her initial impression. What she couldn't erase was the image of Massimo DiLuca's dark chocolate-brown eyes, revealed once he had removed his sunglasses in the pastry shop. And the sheen on his lips from the honey-drizzled *sebada*...

She had expected to have a day to herself before meeting him, to prepare herself emotionally. The term *reclusive* could have so many different connotations, she had thought when her boss had first told her about the assignment. Yes, the baron had agreed to be interviewed about the DiLucas' thriving resort business, the *baronessa* Silvia's upcoming birthday and the official opening of the DiLuca Cardiac Research Center. But perhaps he was doing so reluctantly and would be difficult to work with. She could very well be going to fairy-tale surroundings but dealing with an absolute ogre.

After seeing a rare photo of him online, Ella's pulse had quickened. The photo was from a black-tie event the baron and his wife had attended, and only her back had been visible, but he'd been captured fully by the photographer. The look of him—beardless, black tux and wine glass in hand—had caused a reaction in her that was probably typical of most women when they saw him or came into his sphere... And there was nothing ogre-like about him. At least not physically.

Well, she was in his sphere now. And his manner wasn't ogre-like, either. Granted, her initial impression of him hadn't been the most positive one but was understandable, given his abrupt manner and the way his cap and beard had concealed his identity.

Taking a deep breath, Ella opened up her carry-on and retrieved a short nightie and took it with her to the spacious gold-and-crystal-accented washroom, where she was relieved to be able to finally take a shower. As she lathered with the lilac-scented soap, Ella's thoughts replayed moments from the time the baron had appeared at the airport up to the time he had shown her to her room.

Massimo's manner and tone had seemed different when she had returned from the balcony. Somewhat cooler… Perhaps he had been a little annoyed by her exuberance over her view and room. Could it be Sardinian women were more reserved with their emotions? She shook her head. What did she know? The sole Sardinian she had ever come in contact with had been her father, and that had been for only the first four years of her life.

Well, soon enough, she'd be on the baron's private island, staying in his guesthouse, and interviewing him up close and personal. And her instinct was telling her that she'd be learning much more about him. Maybe more than he wanted her to know…

Ella stepped out of the shower and quickly towel dried her hair and body. She slipped on

ROSANNA BATTIGELLI   49

her nightie and wrapped the provided bathrobe around her. It didn't take long for her hair to air dry on the balcony while she enjoyed the view. Moments later, she was lying between the luxurious cotton sheets, sighing with pleasure before feeling her eyelids get heavier.

"This is living the life," she murmured, smiling. She felt so pampered, and as she began to drift contentedly toward sleep, Ella wondered if this was how a *baronessa* felt...

The ringtone on his phone told Massimo he was getting a text. He stretched to get his phone on his night table and read Ella's message.

I'm almost ready. I'm just on my way to the breakfast room for a quick cappuccino.

He texted back.

Va bene. I will meet you there in a few minutes.

He thought about his dinner the night before. He had wondered if Ella would be joining him and trying her first traditional Sardinian dish, a seafood *fregula* with saffron broth. He had also ordered a local wine, but the *signo-*

rina had not shown up. She must have been exhausted. It had been over thirty degrees Celsius yesterday. Perhaps that was why her cheeks had been flushed so often.

Massimo's thoughts shifted to the baby photo Gregoriu had texted him last night, followed by the same feeling of sadness he always seemed to get recalling how, since his wife had not been able to conceive, they had just agreed to explore adoption possibilities a week before she passed.

He leaped out of bed, willing himself to suppress any further thoughts in that direction. He showered quickly and changed into a pair of white pants and a salmon-colored shirt. He chose a wide-brimmed hat from his selection on the top shelves of his walk-in closet, and putting his sunglasses in his shirt pocket, he took the stairs instead of the elevator to the terrace floor.

Now that he was in his own resort, Massimo didn't have to be concerned about anonymity. The tourists wouldn't know who he was and his employees all knew not to address him by his last name in front of the guests. Entering the room, he scanned the tables and spotted Ella by the far railing, gazing out at the sea, her cappuccino in hand. He strode toward her, thinking what a perfect picture she made wearing a white eyelet blouse over a long, flowered skirt with a matching red belt, her hair held back by a red band.

The warm morning breeze was ruffling her hair and skirt, and she turned moments before Massimo reached her table. It gave him an unexpected jolt. She looked so…refreshed, her glossy red lips parting slightly before smiling a greeting.

"*Buongiorno, signorina* Ross," he said, nodding. "*Prego*, please." He gestured toward her chair. She sat down and took a sip of her cappuccino, leaving a red imprint on her cup and a bit of froth on her lip. She casually licked it off, and at that moment, she looked across at him. He shifted slightly and said a few words to the passing waitress, who nodded with a smile.

He turned back to Ella. She was looking at him with raised brows.

"I was speaking to her in my Sardinian dialect," he explained. "By the way, *signorina*, there is no such thing as a 'quick cappuccino' here. We like to take things nice and slow. I suggest you let go of your North American ways while you're in Sardinia."

He paused as the waitress returned, accompanied by a waiter. She set down an espresso for Massimo and another cappuccino for Ella and a dish for each of them. The waiter placed an oval platter in the middle of the table with divided sections of assorted breakfast pastries—including *sebadas* and *amaretti*—and various cheeses, cold cuts and fruit.

"Mamma mia!" Ella said. "I didn't expect—"

"—to eat?" Massimo lifted an eyebrow. "I hope you are not on a diet. There are so many Sardinian dishes you need to try while you're here."

"I don't diet," she said. "I'm actually a very healthy eater. I wasn't hungry a little while ago, but now, seeing this feast before my eyes—" she picked up her fork "—my mouth is watering!"

Massimo nodded curtly. "It's unfortunate you weren't able to enjoy your first Sardinian dinner last night. I guess you were very jet-lagged."

Ella gave him a sheepish smile and then let out a chuckle. He raised an eyebrow.

"Yes, I was very jet-lagged," she said, as she fixed her plate. "But I had a good sleep and I'll feel even more energized after this lovely breakfast."

He watched her cut up her cantaloupe and prosciutto and then spear it with a fork. *"Buon appetito,"* he nodded. "Enjoy."

Massimo fixed himself a generous plate before asking the waiter to bring some bottled water and a pitcher of freshly squeezed orange juice. Ella didn't seem to be aware of his fleeting glances at her as they ate.

"I think this is a good time to be frank with you, Ella." *Now was as good a time as ever to get something off his mind.*

CHAPTER FOUR

ELLA FINISHED HER cappuccino and set it down. She met his stare, her hands clasped together under her chin. Had she committed a faux pas? Breached some kind of Sardinian breakfast protocol?

Her breath caught in her throat. He was damned good-looking, with his perfect set of teeth and lips, mesmerizing eyes with their rim of thick lashes and dark hair with wavy tips that she could tell were still damp from his shower... *Full stop!*

Mortified where her thoughts were heading, Ella diverted her attention to the platter and chose a couple of *amaretti* before facing him again. *What did he have to be frank with her about?*

"It's nothing personal," he said gruffly. "But I wasn't too happy about doing this set of interviews."

"Um, well, my boss *had* mentioned you

weren't pleased about the original plans," she said with a slight shrug.

"*That* would have been a circus," he said curtly. "I didn't want my home to be invaded by an army of reporters and photographers."

"And it won't be," Ella said lightly. "The army is down to one soldier. *Me.*"

"Which I agreed to—" he nodded with a twist of his lips "—because I want to make my mother happy."

"But *you're* not happy."

"It's…complicated," he said, his eyes piercing into her as if he were trying to decide if he should explain further.

"Look, *signor* DiLuca, I plan to follow the conditions you specified in the contract with my boss. I interview you in the morning, the afternoon is my own to work on the piece, and later on, I interview your mother at her villa after the renovations are done. Any photos I take will be viewed and approved by you before I send them to my boss." She raised her eyebrows. "Oh, and I stay in your guesthouse to avoid having you go back and forth from your island every day." She held out her hands. "Did I miss anything?"

"No." He leaned back, crossing his arms.

"So?" Ella cocked her head. "What exactly is…the problem?" She had almost said "your problem," which would have sounded rude and inappropriate. But she was starting to feel the heat and just wanted Massimo to get to the point.

"I am aware of your achievements," he said, "and your ability to communicate in Italian, which is what I wanted, as my mother isn't proficient in English." His eyes narrowed. "My mother has gone through a long period of—*lutto*—you know, when my father died."

"Mourning." Ella nodded, her voice softening. He wasn't mentioning his own situation, but she imagined he was inferring the same.

"Yes. And just in these past few months, she has started to allow herself to enjoy living again. I just want to make sure that you understand and can be sensitive to my mother, who may have moments of sadness, even now. She needs someone who understands loss."

Something twisted in Ella's chest, an unexpected hurt that the man sitting across from her would assume she had limited life experience and would question her sensitivity and understanding about loss. *How judgmental!* She felt the hurt give way to mingled disappointment and a flash of anger. Feeling a sizzle in her chest, she leaned toward him on the table, her arms crossed in front of her.

"Please allow me to clarify something, *si-*

gnor DiLuca," she said succinctly. "I understand loss and grief quite well." She paused, struck by a wave of emotion but determined to maintain her composure. "But in any case, I haven't gotten to where I am today without being professional above all else. And that includes being sensitive."

What a colossal fool he was. He had seen her eyelids shuttering as if she had been suddenly struck with temple pain, flutter briefly, then open, the vulnerability replaced by an assertive steeliness. He had touched a nerve, but there was no way she was going to display her emotions. His gut feeling told him that he needed to do some damage control.

"I'm sorry if I have offended you, Ella. I was wrong to have judged you because of your age." He cleared his throat. "And I'm sorry for...for the loss you have experienced. It seems I dislike it when others presume to know me and my life without having the full facts, yet I have just done the same to you."

He inhaled deeply. Losing Rita had aged him, aged his heart. And although Ella hadn't shared any details about her loss, he should have known better than to make assumptions about her past experience.

"I hope you can forgive me for *my* insensitivity," he said. His gaze locked with hers, and he hoped she could see the sincerity in his eyes.

Ella drew in a deep breath and let it out slowly. "I suppose I can try to do that," she murmured.

He raised his eyebrows.

"Okay, I can do that," she said more decisively with a toss of her head.

"Thank you," he said, one corner of his mouth lifting. He glanced at his watch. "I'm ready to leave anytime you are."

Massimo felt some of the tension in his shoulders dissipating as his speedboat glided away from the dock, and when the way was clear, he cruised toward one of the distant small islands scattered like a rosary chain in the sea. He couldn't wait to get there and relax with a long, cool drink. The morning had been somewhat intense. And maybe he'd go for an afternoon swim. But first, he'd show Ella to his guesthouse. He imagined she would probably like to settle in and maybe organize her work area. The guesthouse was on a lower slope and situated a hundred and fifty feet from the villa. It overlooked a cove with a small beach of its own.

Since his stay in the guesthouse while the villa was being constructed, no one else had occupied it, not even his mother when she visited. She found the trek to the villa difficult with her arthritic knees and chose to stay in one of the villa's spare rooms.

Massimo had been reluctant to go along with his mother's original plans for the series of interviews, cringing at the thought of being at her place with a team of photographers and reporters from *Living the Life* magazine, not to mention the many friends she wanted to invite along with their eligible daughters. She hadn't been that subtle about getting him out in public again, and he had adamantly refused, only leading her to assume a hurt demeanor.

It was enough, he had told her, that he would be present at the official opening of the Di-Luca Cardiac Research Center the day after her birthday and would not be leaving it to her alone.

Much as Massimo was tempted to stay out of the media spotlight, his conscience wouldn't allow him to shirk his responsibility as a baron. His family had engaged in philanthropic projects contributing to the public good for as long as he could remember, and it would not be right for him, as the current baron and one of the Cardiac Center's benefactors, to be absent at the official opening. He had been the one to conceive of the endeavor and to put together an international team to see to every aspect of its development.

His mother had been on board from the start, and she had been touched by the fact that through Massimo's initiative, and the Di-Lucas' massive financial commitment to the project, the Center would be a world leader in cardiac research, benefitting millions of people. A charitable venture to honor her husband and Massimo's father, and Massimo's wife.

It would be the first public appearance Massimo would be making since Rita's passing. And the Center would be one of the main interview topics *Living the Life* magazine wanted to highlight in their August issue.

Finally, Massimo and his mother had reached a compromise: he would consent to participating in an interview with only one journalist, who would spend the week in his guesthouse, and his mother's birthday event would be at her villa with her close friends minus their eligible daughters.

So, to prepare for Ella's visit, Massimo had the place professionally cleaned, the spacious pantry and restaurant-sized refrigerator fully stocked, and the bedroom and washroom refreshed with new linens and towels. Along with a few scented soaps and bath items, made with local products like juniper, saffron and olive oil.

The house was a two-story structure with a bedroom loft and en suite bathroom and a separate office. The main floor consisted of an open-concept kitchen, dining and living area, with floor-to-ceiling windows facing the cove and endless stretch of turquoise sea. Massimo had wanted to distract himself from his constant grief during the year that he'd be in the guesthouse, and he had spared no expense in indulging himself. The floors were of Orosei marble from Sardinia's east coast, and the modern furnishings were also locally made from the most sought-after craftsmen.

Massimo had also enjoyed perusing a number of antiquarian shops, their owners often showing him unique pieces in private rooms. One item was a decorative sword said to have belonged to a Moorish prince, and a pair of ornate wine goblets had been identified as originating from somewhere in fifteenth-century Iberia, most likely Spain. Sardinia had been part of the Kingdom of Aragon, which was modern-day Spain.

The walls of the kitchen were painted the lightest shade of lemon. The high-end appliances gleamed against a backsplash of hand-painted tiles, which Massimo had commissioned based on those he had seen in paintings of his ancestors. And the curved peninsula, topped by a nine-foot slab of pink granite from the Gallura countryside, was a chef's dream. And it included a chef—if Ella wanted—or she could cook up something herself. The kitchen had double doors that led out to a courtyard with huge terra-cotta planters overflowing with herbs, tomatoes and other vegetables. One section had a decorative pergola with clusters of grapes growing all around it.

Massimo stole a glance at his guest. She was sitting forward in her seat, totally absorbed in the views around her. The breeze made her hair flick around her face and her dress flare up around her legs. With those sunglasses she was wearing, coral-red lipstick, and long skirt with a red belt and headband, she looked like a classic film star. Innocent and *hot* at the same time.

He groaned. Why were his thoughts veering in that direction?

Because you're normal? his inner voice said mockingly.

"Really?" he said aloud.

"I didn't say anything," Ella replied. "It must have been a mermaid whispering in your ear." And then she *giggled*.

Massimo flashed her a look of concern. Where had that comment come from? She wasn't wearing a hat. Could the midday sun have given her sunstroke?

"Have some bottled water, *signorina*. It's in the cooler bag behind my seat."

"I thought I mentioned you can call me Ella."

"Like *Cinderella*?" he said with a chuckle.

"No, actually, it's, um, it's just Ella." She glanced away. "Oh, look at the beach! Is that pink sand?!"

"It is. It's produced by coral when it's broken down, and the currents nudge the grains onto the shore instead of pushing them out to sea."

"Wow. This is such an enchanting place. There's so much I'd like to explore once I've done the interview"

"Oh?" Massimo glanced quickly at her. "You're not going back home right away?"

Ella smiled enigmatically. "I have my holidays after the interview, so I decided to extend my stay for a week."

"I see." For a few moments Massimo concentrated on navigating through the deep blue waters around a series of tiny uninhabited islands and limestone crags. "So where are you staying?"

Ella shrugged and almost looked uncomfortable at his question. "I haven't booked a spot yet. I didn't have time to do a lot of research before I arrived, so I figured I'd decide while I was here. I might stay in the Cagliari area or head north to the Maddalena Islands." She gazed wistfully into the distance. "And then there's the Emerald Coast. It sounds so enchanting when you say it in Italian... *La Costa Smeralda*. And I'll probably visit the island of Caprera..."

"Ah, the island of Garibaldi, the much loved—or resented—icon of Italy's 1861 unification."

"I'm fascinated by Italy. I lucked out getting this assignment."

"From what I understand, it wasn't luck at all," he said. "It was your talent. *And* your ability to speak Italian." His mouth twitched. "*Allora, parliamo italiano?* As they say, 'When in Sardinia...'"

CHAPTER FIVE

ELLA NODDED AT Massimo's request for them to speak in Italian. His accented English was rather pleasant, but when he spoke in his native Italian or regional Sardinian dialect, it seemed to ignite some kind of visceral reaction in her. Like now.

His voice was deep, sonorous, and evoked his island heritage. A heritage they shared...

So why hadn't she revealed that to him when he had asked her about her name? Told him her full name was actually Marinella Rossi? And she had changed it to Ella Ross during a period of angst and rebellion in her late teens, conflicted as to why her birth mother had given her up for adoption and wanting to reject anything that had originated from her Sardinian past, even though it was her adoptive parents who had named her.

Reflecting on it as an adult, Ella had realized she had been struggling with her identity at that time and had attempted to create a new one, starting with a name change. And then one day, finding some old photographs taken when Ella was a child, which her mother had put away in a drawer, Ella's curiosity about her heritage had been aroused. She had started to ask questions, and she knew her mother was pleased, finally able to share details that Ella had previously shown no interest in.

Ella had been devastated when her adoptive mother passed away suddenly from a heart attack a year ago. There were so many things she would have liked to ask, so much she had wanted to say to the woman who had been a loving mother from the start, even during Ella's challenging years. As she mourned her loss, Ella vowed that one day she would return to Sardinia, the place where her parents had met, fallen in love, married and adopted her. And maybe even find her birth mother...

"Ecco! Stiamo arrivando!"

Massimo's words shook her out of her reverie. She had been gazing at the passing scenery for a while without really seeing it. And now they were approaching his island, a sphere of lush green, ringed with white. Ella couldn't make out the actual villa, but a couple of minutes later, she caught glimpses of its light apricot exterior between the feathery boughs of mixed pines and cypresses. The beach, which had seemed like a thin strip as they approached, was in fact a wide band of the whitest sand Ella had ever seen, and the water lapping up against it was a heady mix of turquoise and sea green, sparkling under the rays of the midafternoon sun.

She glanced at Massimo as he idled the boat up to the dock. She hadn't been unaware of the way he looked—and fit—in those white pants and salmon-colored shirt; her pulse had leaped as soon as she had seen him approach her table on the terrace. She had immediately downplayed her involuntary reaction in her mind, telling herself that when she had turned around from gazing at the stunning view, she hadn't expected to see him right there, only a few feet away.

Ella suddenly realized that the speedboat's rumble had subsided. And that Massimo had turned and caught her staring at him. She was relieved she had her sunglasses on…

"Benvenuta a Villa Serena," he said, a brief smile accompanying his welcome. He held out his hand to help her step out of the boat. "You have lovely shoes, Ella," he said, switching back to English, "but I hope you also brought a practical pair for the beach and for the path between the guesthouse and the villa. It's un-

even in places, and I wouldn't want you to twist your ankle."

Ella felt the strength of his clasp as he helped her. "Thanks," she murmured. "And yes, I brought several pairs of shoes." She watched as he retrieved her suitcase and carry-on. She went to grab the carry-on, but he put up his hand. "I'll take them up. You can concentrate on walking."

Ella followed Massimo to the path beyond the dock, which was parallel to the beach before curving its way between rows of oleander bushes, the sweet scent of their pink blossoms mingling with the sea breeze. What a beautiful backdrop to where she would be conducting her morning interviews with Massimo. She felt a shiver of excitement run through her at the thought of the time she would have after working on her piece to walk barefoot in the sand that resembled icing sugar and then take a dip in those pristine waters.

She stumbled suddenly on a tree root, and Massimo turned at her exclamation, dropped her luggage and leaped to her side, grasping her before she fell. Ella found herself face-planted against his chest instead of the ground, his beard brushing her forehead. Her heart was clanging...or was that *his*?

She closed her eyes momentarily and

breathed in his scent. And then her eyes jerked open. What was she doing? She pulled away awkwardly. "Sorry about that," she blurted. "I should watch where I'm stepping. Especially with these shoes," she added ruefully.

"Tutto bene?" he said, glancing down. "No twisted ankle?"

"All good," she said. "Thank goodness. That would have been horrible. For me *and* for you."

"I think you're still tired and not over your jet lag." His brow furrowed. "The guesthouse is just ahead. I suggest you settle in and relax, have a nap if you wish, and in a few hours, I will come back and show you around. And then after dinner this evening, we can go over the interview schedule. *Va bene, Ella?*"

"Va bene, barone," she said lightly. *"Grazie."*

His eyes narrowed. "The feudal system in Sardinia ended almost two centuries ago. So it is not necessary to address me with this formal title. Besides," he added, his lips curving into a smile, "when you call me *barone* it makes me feel like *I'm* a century old."

"Well, I look forward to finding out about your centuries-old heritage—and maybe some colorful DiLuca ancestors—during our interview tomorrow morning," she said, returning his smile.

* * *

"Welcome to the guesthouse." Massimo looked back and saw Ella's eyes widening as they approached.

"I thought this was Villa Serena," she blurted. "I was expecting a little guesthouse."

He gestured toward a canopy of trees above which they could now glimpse his villa. "I— what's the word—*indulged* myself. I had this guesthouse built first, so I could oversee the day-to-day progress of the villa. I preferred this to a tent." He smiled crookedly, setting down Ella's luggage by the entrance door. "Something that wolves and wild boars couldn't get into."

"What? There are wild animals on this island?" She glanced furtively around her.

He laughed. "I haven't actually seen—or heard—any. My mother insists that I'm the only wild creature here, choosing to live in isolation…" He saw Ella's lips tilt upward tentatively, and he repressed his urge to laugh.

"I can see that you're not sure what you have gotten yourself into," he said wryly, opening the door for her. "But I promise you, Ella, you will be safe." His gaze swept over her. "Especially if you change your shoes."

Massimo waited for her to enter, then he followed with a piece of luggage in each hand. "Where would you like these?"

"Oh, you can leave them right there. I'll bring them later to the bedroom."

"Why don't I just take them now, so that I don't have to worry about you falling on the spiral stairway to the loft?" Without waiting for her to answer, he strode across the foyer to the living area, and looking back over his shoulder, said, "I might as well take you on a quick tour before I disappear into my own cave."

"Um, okay." She glanced around.

"And the fridge is stocked if you would like a beverage or a snack."

"Thank you. That's very thoughtful."

Massimo nodded and headed up the stairway to the second level. He had designed the loft with floor-to-ceiling windows so that it had views of the sea on every side. From the king-size bed, the facade of the villa could be seen over the crowns of the trees. And patio doors on one wall opened to a roomy balcony, flanked on its side by a fig tree that his gardener had planted, along with other fruit trees and flowering bushes.

"Oh, my goodness," Ella said, gazing around her. "I can see why you wanted to stay here. This is about as close as heaven as I can imagine."

Massimo felt a tightening in his stomach at

the mention of heaven. It had been more of a *haven* than heaven at the beginning, a place where he could lose himself in the house plans instead of feeling constantly overwhelmed by grief. But when those dark moments came, when the recurring feelings of shock and disbelief resurfaced, not only during the day but in his dreams, he would seek respite in the perennial rhythms of the island: the ebb and flow of the sea at dawn, gushing at his feet; the silky feel of the white sand as he walked the entire stretch of the beach before it butted up against a granite outcropping, and then he would turn around and do the long trek back to his guesthouse, distract himself with computer work, before embarking on the task of cooking.

During that year of construction, Massimo had turned down his mother's offer of sending one of her chefs over to at least take cooking off his mind. He had wanted nobody around him while he tried to make sense of what had happened in his life and to figure out how he would move forward.

Seeing that Ella had gone to survey the view from the balcony, Massimo turned to look at the bed. The new linens suited the room. He was actually glad to have had the original ones removed, washed and donated to charity. In a way, it was symbolic, starting something new and fresh.

He had spent a long, lonely year in that bed, sometimes tossing all night. But on some nights, he'd sit out on the balcony and gaze up at the star-filled sky or the moon; he'd feel the sheer immensity and mystery of the galaxy, and somehow, it would give him a speck of hope, that Rita was where she was destined to be and so was he. And he realized more and more that the sooner he accepted reality, the sooner he would have peace…

It hadn't hurt, either, that he had consulted a bereavement counselor for a few months. As the head of DiLuca Luxury Resorts, he had always felt confident, in charge when it came to his business. And it wasn't just because it made him billions. He had a genuine love of his island, and he wanted people from all over the world to experience it, to go home with the jeweled sea and enchanting Sardinian landscapes forever in their memory.

But when he'd lost his wife, he had felt as if he had been cast out to sea in a tiny boat with no rudder. During a vicious storm…

The counselor had helped him maneuver slowly but surely toward a sheltered cove, using his sheer will, somehow giving him the strength to battle the angry waves that threatened to crush him.

Now, looking at his bed, the memories of that time resurfaced but without the sharp pang of grief. It was more like a moment of resigned sadness. And it felt strange to imagine someone else sleeping in his bed and sharing dinner with him later...

Now that he was living in the villa, he had hired a personal chef—who also happened to be a close friend—to come over three times a week. His mother had insisted that Massimo dine with Ella every Sunday "to engage with humankind," and the remaining three days, Massimo cooked for himself. Today would have been Angelo's day, but he had another commitment and would be coming the following day instead. So today, Massimo would be cooking...*for two.*

His thoughts were interrupted by the return of Ella, beaming.

"I am very grateful for your generosity in allowing me to stay here," she said, her eyes crinkling at the corners.

Massimo shrugged. "To be honest, I was thinking more about myself and how to get through these interviews with the least disruption to my routine."

Ella's smile diminished. "Well, I appreciate your candor, *signor*—I mean Massimo. I'll make every effort not to be a fly in your ointment. And now, if you don't mind, I'll unpack and leave you to your routine—" she glanced at her watch "—until our meeting later this evening to go over the week's agenda."

CHAPTER SIX

ELLA'S FACE HAD begun to tingle at Massimo's surprising bluntness. And she had responded with a little bluntness of her own.

His forehead creased, but she turned away to avoid any further conversation and walked over to where Massimo had set down her luggage.

She heard his husky *"arrivederci"* and footsteps as he left, and she busied herself emptying the contents of her carry-on on top of the bed. When she glanced out the balcony doors, which she had left open, she caught a glimpse of Massimo's back as he ambled up the incline leading to his villa.

Yes, he had made it clear more than once that he considered the prospective interviews disruptive...

Ultimately he had agreed to them to please or appease his mother, so like it or not, he'd have to put up with a few changes to his routine. And *her*. It wasn't as if she were staying a month; the week would fly by.

Ella transferred the clothes on the bed into the large dresser. After emptying some of the items of her big suitcase into the deep drawers and hanging others in the walk-in closet, she placed the two pieces of luggage into one corner of the closet and made her way to the en suite bathroom.

After a refreshing shower, Ella slipped on her flip-flops and sauntered over to the walk-in closet. She rifled through the dresses she had hung up and decided on a lemon yellow sundress with decorative faux pockets, a lemon-shaped button on each flap.

Feeling reenergized, Ella plugged in her adapter and set up her laptop on the desk in the loft. She attached her earphones and reviewed her list of questions for the next morning's interview while listening to classical music. She tweaked a few queries and added some new ones before going over her notes for the remaining days, including those for the interview with the *baronessa*.

When Ella finished reviewing and amending her comments for the last interview, she turned off the music, shut down her laptop and removed her earphones. She checked the time and gasped. She had been so absorbed with her notes that she hadn't realized that almost three hours had gone by. She started at the sudden knocking at the front door.

The entrance door had been left open, and Massimo's *"Buona sera"* carried easily from the screen door to the loft.

"I came by an hour ago and called out to see if you cared to join me for a tour around the villa and a bite to eat, but I guess you didn't hear me," he said loudly.

"Come in. I'll be right there." Ella ran her fingers through her hair and quickly descended the spiral staircase.

"Don't rush. We're on island time," he said, his mouth quirking.

Ella grabbed the railing. "Oh, my," she said, closing her eyes. "I just felt dizzy." She let her head lean against the post.

She stiffened slightly at the feel of his arm around her shoulder seconds later.

"Let me help you to the couch," he said brusquely. "You should have some water. And something to eat." His brow furrowing, he added, "I have a feeling you haven't acquainted yourself yet with the refrigerator."

When Massimo started to guide Ella into the living area, she was overcome by another wave of dizziness. She felt herself starting to swirl and slide as if in slow motion, and ended up in a swing of some sort. When she opened her eyes, she saw that the swing was actually Massimo's arms carrying her to the couch.

"Don't move," he ordered, setting her down gently. He watched her for a few moments, his eyes pinned on her. Then he nodded. "I'll be back with some water."

Ella had no intention of moving. She would see how she felt once she had a drink. So much for their meeting in his office to discuss the interview schedule, which he had drawn up and emailed to her a few days before her flight. Well, she couldn't see *that* happening tonight. It would soon be dusk, and lovely though the island might be, Ella wasn't thrilled with the idea of walking back to the guesthouse alone after the interview. She hadn't been able to tell if he was actually joking about the wild boars and the wolves...

Ella sat up slowly as Massimo came back holding a tray with a tall glass of water and a platter of cold meats, cheeses and fruit. She couldn't help looking at the muscled arms that had swept her up and carried her across the room moments ago. Imagining herself flopped against his chest ignited a thrumming in her own chest.

"Ecco l'acqua," he said as he set down the

tray on the circular coffee table. "Have a drink. It will help clear your head."

Ella nodded and took the glass. She had a few sips and was about to put it down, when Massimo urged her to keep drinking. "You could be dehydrated," he said. "It was hot and you didn't have a hat on the way here. And if it's not that, it could be that you've gone hours without eating. No wonder you're dizzy."

He gestured toward the platter as he sat in the accent chair opposite her. *"Prego."*

"Oh, my goodness, this can't be all for me."

"It could be, but if you'd rather share…"

"Of course." She looked at the selection of cheeses and slices of salami and prosciutto. "Are these home—?"

"Made by my mother," he said with a crooked smile.

"Your *mother*?" Ella had to stop her jaw from dropping. His mother was co-owner of a billion-dollar resort business. Why would *she* be doing this kind of work?

"It is hard to believe, I know. *Prego*," he said, indicating for her to help herself, and then he prepared his own panino. "Mamma loves to cook. She does have a personal chef or two, but she likes to prepare a lot of food that her parents and grandparents made themselves. 'Someone has to keep our family traditions going' she tells me all the time." He gave a deep laugh. "So she will return home from a long board meeting, and a little while later, she will be in the kitchen, preparing *sebadas*, or *spinaci al pecorino*, or *purpugia*—"

"What is it? The last thing you said."

Massimo's eyebrows shot up. "It's a pork dish that's marinated and—how do you say—*saltata in padella*?"

"Sautéed. What kind of marinade?"

"Is this part of an interview, or are you actually interested?" he said, leaning forward.

Ella bit her lip. Noticing the slight rolling of his eyes, she suspected that he didn't want to waste his time with someone who was faking an interest in what he was saying.

"I'm *very* interested," she said quickly. "I would like to know more about Sardinian cooking. My father—" She froze and stared back at Massimo, her mind scrambling to think of a way to answer. *Another near slip.*

"Your father…?"

"Um, yes, my late father…liked to cook. And I…like to cook, too," she finished weakly.

His jaw relaxed and she caught a flash of empathy in his eyes. "*Va bene*, I'll tell you. You chop some herbs and crush some spices into a bowl with garlic, white wine and vinegar. We use sage, rosemary, mint, bay leaves, fennel seeds and black peppercorns. You put the sliced meat in the marinade for one or two days, turning the meat over. And then you remove the slices, pat them dry and cook the meat in a skillet with olive oil."

He looked directly at Ella as he kissed the fingers of his right hand in the way that Italians expressed their pleasure at food or anything else. The gesture made her nerve endings tingle. For a couple of seconds, she allowed herself to be stuck in his gaze, realizing how sensual his eyes really were, with that dark rim around them. She wondered if the trait came from the Spanish or Moorish influence in the island's history.

Ella forced herself to break away from her trance-like state. "That sounds so aromatic, with all those herbs," she said, reaching for her glass. She drank the rest of her water and checked the time on her watch. "Thank you for the food," she said. "Everything was so good. I will thank your mother personally when I meet her."

"Which will be on Sunday," he drawled, before popping a piece of fontina cheese in his mouth.

Ella frowned. "But I thought I read in the email that Sunday was your day off?"

"It is. And it's tradition for me to go over to my mother's villa for dinner."

"Well... I don't want to intrude on your family traditions."

Massimo's lips curved slightly. "You are the guest of the DiLucas for one week, and so for one week you will join us in our traditions, big and small. And knowing my mother, she will be sure to—" he stroked his beard "—how do you say it? Oh yes, cook up a...a storm."

Ella flashed him a smile. Her face had a flush to it now, unlike earlier, when she had felt dizzy. Her pallor had been noticeable when she had first come down the stairs, but when she had slumped against the post, his adrenalin had jackknifed and he had leaped to her side, his heart clanging against his ribs. And when she had another spell moments later, he had scooped her up immediately to prevent her from falling.

In the kitchen, he had grabbed a pitcher of water from the refrigerator and poured some into two glasses. He drank his first, trying to steady his heart from the shock of seeing a replay of his wife passing out. And then he had wasted no time in getting the tray that he had had prepared for Ella. She needed water and nourishment. *Immediately.*

The *panino* and water had helped. Her color had returned and apparently her spirit, as well.

He stood up and checked his watch. "There's really no point in going over the interview schedule tonight. Why don't you just relax for the rest of the evening? There's actually a guest bedroom on this floor. I'd feel much better if you slept down here." He glanced up at the staircase leading to the loft. "I wouldn't want you to have another dizzy spell, Ella."

"I feel fine, now that I've had something to drink and eat," she said with a shrug. "You don't have to worry about me."

"That's where you're wrong," Massimo said crisply. "You're a guest on my island. Therefore, I'm responsible for *you*. And for your safety."

He saw Ella's eyebrows arch and caught a flicker of indecision when she followed his gaze back to the stairwell.

"Maybe you should just stay in a guest room at my villa for tonight," he said, stroking his chin. "Or, you can stay *here* but *I* will sleep in the guest room on this floor. Either way, I'll be close by, in case you need me."

He saw Ella's eyes flicker with…surprise? Suspicion? Good heavens, was she thinking…? Of course she might think it. She was alone on an island with a billionaire whose reputation she knew little or nothing about. For all she knew, he was a rake who was using her dizziness as an excuse to manipulate the situation by pretending to be concerned for her health and safety.

"Look, *signorina*," he said, feeling he needed to address her with some formality. "You don't have to worry. There's a Moorish sword displayed on one wall in your room. You can easily remove it to defend yourself if you feel the need." His mouth twitched, but he could see that she wasn't amused. Or convinced.

"I'm sorry. I don't want you to be uncomfortable. I think it's better if you just stay here, and I will stretch out on the chaise lounge on the beach. If you are not feeling well, you just need to call me from your balcony overlooking the cove. I just want to make sure you will be okay tonight," he added in what he hoped was a gentle tone, but it came out sounding gruff.

Ella gaped at him. "But…what if a wolf or wild boar—?"

He burst out laughing. "Let me reassure you, Ella, there are no wolves on my island. As for wild boars—" he shrugged "—my ancestors sometimes had to fight them with bare hands." His eyes narrowed. *And I've had to fight worse demons*. He felt a tightening in his chest. "But those ancestors all survived."

He stood up brusquely. "The only wild boar we will encounter on this island is the one from the market, served for dinner in a *ragù*. I will accompany you up the stairs, Ella, and then I will leave you to enjoy my night under the stars."

CHAPTER SEVEN

DECIDING THAT HIS dark eyes were sincere, Ella made her way carefully up the spiral stairway and walked slowly into her room, her gaze landing on the Moorish sword. A shiver ran through her, not because of fear, but because of the sense of mystery around Massimo DiLuca.

Changing into a nightgown, she thought about the man in whose company she had been for less than two days. Yet in that short time, she had glimpsed different sides to him. He was a good son, had shown Ella his generosity and sense of humor, concern and empathy, but there was also an intensity about him that she suspected he kept in check.

Perhaps it was a trait he had inherited from his wild boar-wrestling Sardinian ancestors. She had a sudden image of him in a torn linen shirt, his muscled chest and forearms glistening with perspiration, his eyes blazing with passion as he confronted a charging boar.

Oh. My. God. What was she doing? This was not good. *No, no, no.* She had to get these kinds of thoughts out of her mind. Get this Sardinian out of her mind. At least in that way…

Good luck with that, an inner voice chuckled. *He's hardly like your last boyfriend. This one is a man who's willing to sleep outside to make sure you're okay during the night.*

Ella's pulse quickened. She turned off the light and walked to the open balcony doors. The sky looked like a blue-black quilt speckled with clusters of stars. Ella caught her breath. They looked so close… The half-moon, suspended jauntily at an angle, was reflected in the waters of the cove, undulating ripples, their gentle swoosh on the shore sounding like a meditation app she had sometimes listened to.

Her gaze shifted to the outdoor furniture set farther back from the beach on a large landscaped area with a diagonally tiled section. Massimo was lying back on a cushioned chaise lounge with his hands joined behind his neck, staring out at the water. He must have grabbed a throw on his way out; it was bunched up against his leg.

He was actually going to sleep outside.

Either he was crazy or just a hell of a nice guy.

Watching Massimo in the dark gave her

a strange feeling. What if he looked up and saw her? Ella turned away and went over to lie down on the bed. The breeze was strong enough to reach her, but it was pleasant. She would probably not need the bed covers tonight.

But how could she possibly fall asleep when the man—the billionaire—she would be interviewing tomorrow had decided to camp out on a chaise lounge outside his guesthouse, just because he was concerned about her?

Ella shifted to one side of the bed. At times she had wondered what it would be like to have a partner, someone you trusted with your secrets and your life. But those thoughts hadn't lingered. Her goal was to be the best that she could at her chosen career, and unless her future forever man was able to put stars in her eyes, she had reasoned to herself, then her work would continue to be her focus.

Ella flipped her pillow over and, after a few restless minutes, felt her eyelids starting to droop. The mattress was perfect...

Her eyes flew open. How could she allow herself to sleep when Massimo was sacrificing his comfort for her? She turned to view the sky. And the stars, which seemed even brighter now. Sighing, she rolled out of bed and padded to the balcony.

Peering down, she saw that he had turned to one side, his arms crossed at his chest. He had fallen asleep.

A warm feeling of tenderness washed over her, followed by a hint of guilt. She couldn't let him stay there the whole night.

"Massimo," she called out.

He leaped out of the chaise and looked up. "Are you all right? Are you dizzy again?"

"No, I'm fine. It's just... I can't let you sleep all night out there." She paused. "So if you intend on staying, then...you might as well stay in the guest room. That way, at least we'll both get some rest."

For a few moments Massimo didn't respond, and Ella wished she could see his face out of the shadows.

"Va bene," he said huskily. "I am glad you are okay. *Buona notte."*

Ella watched as he grabbed the throw and disappeared into the shadows.

She glanced up at the sky and felt a knot form in her throat. When she was young and missing her father, her mother would gently tell her that he was in a place called heaven, where there were many beautiful angels and that when she looked up at a sky full of stars, it was their wings sparkling, and he was close by...

She got back into bed and realized that she

had left her bedroom door partially open. She thought about closing it and then decided against it. Massimo DiLuca would not be intruding on her privacy. He had already shown a selflessness that had stunned her, reinforcing her gut feeling he was a man of integrity and honor.

Ella pulled the light bedsheet over her, leaving her arms uncovered. It was strange to think of sleeping under the same roof as this enigmatic baron, and just as strange to think about being in the same bed that he had slept in.

She heard some movements and felt her pulse quicken. And then she heard his footsteps receding and a door opening and shutting. Closing her eyes, she willed herself to fall asleep. They would be meeting tomorrow morning, and she wanted to appear alert and articulate. And in the afternoon when she was on her own, she'd go online and book a place to stay once her interview sessions were over. She had decided that it made sense to find a place in Posada, where her uncle still lived and where her father came from.

It was a heady feeling, knowing that she was finally back in Sardinia and could soon be connecting with an uncle who had been part of her early life. Maybe he could shed some light—if he knew anything at all—about the mother—no, *woman*—who had given her up for adoption.

And maybe help Ella to find her.

In any case, Ella considered only one person her mother, and that was the one who had chosen her. *Cassandra*.

If she ever had children, she would name her little girl Cassandra. And call her Cassie, too. And if she had a boy, she would give him her father's name. She wouldn't use the English version of Michael. No, she would keep it Micheli, to honor the Sardinian man who had adopted her and loved her for four years, before...

Ella's eyes welled up. The photos her mother had of those years were precious to her. She had gone over them so many times with Cassandra, who had shared them with Ella from the time she was able to understand, telling her how much her *papà* had loved her and how he had taken her everywhere: to the piazza for a jaunt, sitting on his shoulders; to his parents' farm to pick olives; to the sea for an early-morning swim; or to the countryside for a picnic. One of Ella's favorite photos was one a family member had taken of her parents, smiling as they both held her between them, as they celebrated her fourth birthday, her last with her father...

"Oh, *papà*, I've come home," she whispered, dabbing her eyes with the edge of the bedsheet.

Massimo took off his shirt and pants and tossed them on top of a chair. Now that he was in the guesthouse, he might as well be comfortable. He opened the shutters of the large window and stretched out on the bed, the half-moon lending the room some illumination.

His heartbeat had settled down after rocketing twice in the last few hours. Ella Ross had given him quite the scare. First with her dizzy spell, and just a few minutes ago when she had called him from the balcony. Thank goodness that she hadn't experienced another episode. Still, he wondered if he should arrange for her to see a doctor... He'd ask her tomorrow.

He breathed in and out deeply. The breeze was refreshing after the heat of the day, and he would have been comfortable enough outside, but he couldn't say that he was disappointed to be spending the night in this king-size bed. After the jolt of hearing Ella call his name, he had been genuinely surprised at her comment.

So, she trusted him...

The last thing he had expected today was to be spending the night in his guesthouse. With his Canadian guest. And although she had consented to having him sleep inside, he imagined that she might be feeling a little awkward, as he was.

She wasn't what he had expected.

He was intrigued by her, actually. He liked the fact she hadn't put on any airs or pretenses. She hadn't tried to impress him, and she had had no problem letting him know how she felt, like when she had shared the fact that she had suffered loss in her life. He had regretted being so judgmental.

When his lifestyle had been more public before the passing of his wife, Massimo had generally observed people found it hard to be themselves around him. Being a billionaire either made people stay away from him, mistakenly thinking themselves as inferior, or they blatantly tried to ingratiate themselves with him.

Ella hadn't shown either tendency. And that put him at ease about the upcoming interviews. He just hoped she wouldn't have any further episodes of dizziness.

He closed his eyes. The sheets felt cool on his bare chest and legs. He wondered if Ella was just as comfortable in his bed. An image flashed in his mind of her face on his pillow, just the way it had been resting against his chest earlier...

Something pulled in his chest. Something that caught Massimo by surprise.

He didn't want to go there.

He redirected his thoughts to a safer place: the next day's agenda. He was to have shown up at the guesthouse at 9:00 a.m., accompany Ella to his villa, offer her a cappuccino and biscotti and then proceed to his study for the first official interview.

But since he was already at the guest-house, he would take the liberty of preparing espresso and cappuccino for them the next morning. And the refrigerator and pantry were fully stocked, so he would put together a breakfast tray. That was, if he was up be-fore she was.

He paused. This all sounded so...so inti-mate, the way a man would act for his lady or vice versa. But, he reasoned to himself, there was no point leaving in the morning only to return a while later. And there was no reason that they couldn't deal with this situation in a professional way.

Since they hadn't gone over the entire week's agenda this evening, they would start with that first thing in the morning. He imagined the in-terview itself would focus on the history of the DiLuca family, its origins, noteworthy ances-tors and the role of a baron throughout the centuries, for starters. That in itself could take the whole day, he mused wryly, let alone a couple of hours or so.

Massimo turned on one side to gaze at the star-dotted sky. A few seconds later, he caught the flash of a falling star. Had Ella seen it? It would have been something, seeing it while outside... He felt a surge of pride and gratitude, living in such a beautiful region. He hoped Ella would be able to enjoy some of it in the week she was here. She had the afternoons to herself, and he had already stated in the letter to her boss that he would arrange for her boat trip back and forth from *Villa Serena* to Sardinia whenever she wanted.

He remembered that Ella would be staying for an additional week. She should really think about booking a place as soon as possible. Sardinia was a prime holiday destination in the summer, and prices would be higher during this peak season, especially in the most popular resort region, the *Costa Smeralda*, if that's where she wanted to stay.

Leaving it this late could make finding a place challenging. He'd diplomatically pose the question of what kind of accommodation she was looking for in the morning. Not that he was interested in knowing her budget, but he could advise her as to some possibilities. He knew many resort owners, and not only ones with high-end establishments.

Massimo heard the sudden high-pitched call of a scops owl, its intermittent cry sounding like a timer going off, and a second, more distant call. He was used to these night sounds, and they generally didn't disturb his sleep. But he wondered if Ella was hearing them now or had already fallen into a deep slumber.

He closed his eyes. He needed to stop thinking about her if he wanted to get a half-decent sleep tonight…

CHAPTER EIGHT

ELLA WOKE UP when her alarm went off. She reached over to stop it and realized that the aroma of coffee had wafted into her room. She sat up and squinted at her surroundings, disoriented for a moment. And then she remembered she wasn't alone. The reclusive Baron DiLuca had spent the night in the guest bedroom. In his own guesthouse. Rubbing her eyes, she got out of bed and padded to the en suite bathroom for a quick shower, aware of the soft drumming in her chest. She still couldn't believe that he had been willing to sleep outside the entire night so he could be around if she felt dizzy again.

Well, she felt absolutely fine now. Refreshed and ready for a cappuccino before heading to Massimo's villa for the first interview. She headed over to the closet and looked for something professional but also light and comfortable.

She chose a pair of tropical-themed palazzo pants and a fuchsia silk top with short sleeves and slanted hemline. She put on a pair of cream wedge sandals and made her way out of the loft and down the spiral staircase.

"*Buongiorno*, Ella." Massimo nodded, his gaze sweeping over her. "Your cappuccino is ready."

"My goodness. I didn't expect to be treated like royalty." She crossed the living room and entered the adjoining kitchen.

Massimo laughed. "You would be an easy queen to please," he said. "Not like the queen bee, who expects to be royally served with honey."

"Well, I don't aspire to such extravagant tastes," she replied with a fluttering of her lashes as she sat at the curved island. "I come from humble beginnings."

"Oh?" Massimo's eyes narrowed as he set down her demitasse. "What exactly is your heritage?"

Ella had a sip of her cappuccino. Why was she always saying things that she regretted? "Um, I'm Canadian."

"Are you sure?" he said, his mouth quirking. "You seemed to hesitate."

Ella laughed uneasily. "Well, you know us Canadians. We have a variety of cultures in our heritage." She reached for a brioche from the plate he had prepared. "Thanks, by the way, for getting all this ready."

Massimo nodded. "*Prego*. I hoped you wouldn't mind."

"It's *your* guesthouse."

"*Sì*, but you're the guest. It's your space now." He raised his eyebrows. "I trust you had a good sleep? The bed was comfortable enough?"

The intensity of his dark eyes and the mention of his bed, where she had imagined him sleeping, caused spears of heat to swirl through her. "Yes, thank you. It was such a beautiful night. The sky was amazing. I've never seen so many stars up there. And I actually saw a shooting star." She stopped, realizing she was rambling.

"Did you make a wish?"

Ella's eyebrows lifted. "Oh, do Italians do that, too?"

"Yes, there is a feast day for a martyr on August tenth, *La Festa di San Lorenzo*. It coincides with a meteor shower, and the falling stars, or *stelle cadenti*, are said to be San Lorenzo's tears." He gazed at her intently. "So did you make a wish, Ella?"

She liked the way her name sounded pronounced the Italian way: lighter and with a slightly longer drawing out of the double *l*. 'Of course," she said. "It's the first time I ever saw one. Maybe that's a good sign."

"Well, I hope you get your wish," he said.

"What about you?"

Massimo gave an enigmatic smile. "I leave the wishing to the kids…and the romantics," he added, eyeing her meaningfully. "I like to believe I create my own destiny."

Ella bit into her brioche. So that's where he was at… "Doesn't it take some of the magic out of life?" she said wonderingly. "I mean, not expecting any surprises to suddenly come your way?"

The crinkling around Massimo's eyes had smoothed out, and his smile had faded. "The surprises of the universe can be quite cruel," he said curtly.

Ella wasn't sure how to respond. Massimo had to be thinking about his late wife. And she wasn't about to venture anywhere near *that* territory. Not that she wasn't empathetic; she just didn't want it to seem like she was digging for information about a subject with sad or traumatic memories.

And she doubted that he wanted to discuss anything about his wife, if the thin line of his lips was any indication. "Well, I suppose we should get started on interview number one," she said lightly.

"If you're finished with your cappuccino, I'll take it, and then we can be on our way," he said, and when she nodded, he leaned forward to grab the cup, but his hand stopped in midair and went instead to her cheek, where he wiped off what she figured was a dollop of custard from her brioche.

Massimo's face was just inches away from hers, and as their eyes locked, Ella was sure that he could hear the accelerated thumping of her heart. She wanted to glance away but somehow couldn't, and seconds later, he was the one who backed off.

Ella stood up, grabbed her handbag, and strode to the door. He caught up to her and held it open, and soon they were walking up a slope made of pavers in the grass that was flanked on both sides by flowering pink and white oleander trees. The scent was sweet and heady, and Ella made a mental note to herself to look for a perfume with that flower essence.

At the ring of his cell phone, Massimo retrieved it from his back pocket and checked the message. He laughed softly. "Look at this," he said, and held out his phone. "Gregoriu and Lia's baby. And here's the one he sent me yesterday."

"Aww, she's so beautiful. And look at all her hair!"

He leaned in to look again, his arm brushing against hers. "She takes after her mother in that department," he said with a laugh, looking up.

Ella smiled, her breath suspended for a moment with his face only inches away from hers. The crinkling at the outer corners of his eyes and his grin were so...so distractingly attractive. When he looked down to reply to the text, without moving away, Ella felt a warmth spreading through her at the proximity of his neck, and the pulse at the base of his throat.

He put his phone away and gestured to Ella to continue walking.

The walkway curved through the last of the oleanders and opened to a view of *Villa Serena*. The path now changed from intermittent paver stones to one of huge granite slabs arranged in a curving design that led right up to the villa entrance.

The grounds were breathtaking. And huge. Ella hoped she could take a better look after the interview. She didn't imagine Massimo was up to giving her a tour now. There were landscaped areas with crescents of yellow, red and pink begonias, a separate rose garden, and a variety of flowering bushes, including giant rosy peonies. And beyond, the Olympic-sized infinity pool that gave the illusion it flowed seamlessly into the chameleon-like sea, shifting from turquoise to midnight blue.

It took her breath away.

This was a wonderland, and Ella was in complete awe of the fact that the man she was walking with had had this paradise created for him. Her gaze shifted to the sprawling stucco villa with arched doorways and windows, ceramic-tiled roof, and outdoor lounge area with thick sprays of violet cascading over a whitewashed wall. It had to be wisteria. So enchanting. And romantic… At least for *her*. Ella felt a wave of sadness, thinking of the baron living here by himself. It was his choosing, of course, but didn't the fact that his wife wasn't there to share it with him emphasize his loss? His grief? He hadn't made any mention of his personal life nor did she expect him to…

Her boss had advised her to avoid any reference to Massimo's wife and her passing, as per the baron's specifications. The latter expected the interview to focus on three things and three things only: the DiLuca Luxury Resort Company, the upcoming opening of the DiLuca Cardiac Research Center and his mother's birthday.

Ella gazed at the man who was walking ahead of her now and felt almost guilty, liking the way he looked in those perfectly fitting white trousers.

You're only human, an inner voice reassured her. *The fact that he's a widower has nothing to do with his appearance. You're allowed to find a man attractive.*

And then he suddenly turned around, causing her arms to instinctively fly up to stop herself from crashing into him. For a moment their eyes locked, and Ella realized her hands were planted flat against his chest.

"Sorry," they said simultaneously, and Ella took a step back, letting her arms fall to her sides.

"You must have been going over the interview questions in your mind," he drawled, the corners of his eyes creasing. "I was informed that you're very skilled at your job. And—how do you say—*focalizzata.*"

Yes, she had been focused all right. *On his backside.*

Ella was sure her cheeks were blazing. *Good God, what a way to start the first day of interviews.*

Massimo led Ella through the marble foyer and then an arched doorway to his study. He gestured for her to sit in one of the armchairs and he sat opposite her. The arched windows looked out to a clear view of the sea, and he enjoyed spending his work hours here, with the salty breeze wafting in and nothing but blue sea and sky in his line of vision.

She was taking in the view now, and as he observed her profile, he realized with a jolt that she was the first woman, other than his mother, to have set foot on his island and in *Villa Serena*. When they had entered minutes ago, he had suggested to Ella that they get started with business, and then he would take her for a tour—if she liked—later.

Massimo knew quite well there were a few unattached socialites—mostly daughters of his mother's friends—who would like nothing better than for him to show an interest and invite them over. He couldn't help being a little cynical, wondering if it was their anticipation of winning his favor and ending up enjoying a lifestyle even more opulent than the one they already had or if they actually cared about knowing him as someone other than the billionaire resort magnate.

He wasn't in a hurry to get involved. In the three years since his wife passed, he had gone through all the heart-and mind-wrenching stages of grief, and this past year, could say to himself that he had accepted the reality of his loss and was ready to move forward. Even if it was at the pace of a snail...

He saw Ella turning away from the view. She pulled her recording device out of her handbag and set it on the accent table between them.

"Why don't we go over the schedule for the week before we begin?" he said, reaching for the papers on his desk nearby.

"Of course, since we didn't get that done yesterday," she said ruefully. "I have it on my laptop."

"Non c'è problema," he said. "It won't take long. And no need to open up your laptop. I printed off copies of the file."

Massimo handed her a page with the schedule. He hadn't been thrilled about doing the interviews, but now that Ella had arrived, he was anxious to get started. He went over the timetable for their morning sessions and the times for the ones she would be doing with his mother. When they were done, he placed the file on his desk and sat back in his office chair.

"Allora, cominciamo?" This morning's session would be about the DiLuca family history and how his late father had started the resort business.

"Yes, let's begin," Ella said, nodding, and

turned on the device. "First of all, thank you for allowing me to record these interviews." She smiled. "Tell me about your ancestors, *signor* DiLuca. How far back can you trace your lineage?"

He leaned back in his armchair. He explained that his earliest known ancestor had been an enterprising merchant who had amassed a fortune in two areas: silk and spices. It was passed on from generation to generation that this Federico DiLuca had begun with raising his own small collection of silkworms, keeping them munching happily on mulberry leaves. He had boldly traveled to China and had reputedly brought his fine silks to the court of Genghis Khan, who commissioned him to be a regular provider. Before too long, Federico was doing a brisk trade on the Silk Road.

"That's very intriguing," Ella said, jotting notes down on a pad, despite the fact she was recording. "Was Federico married?"

"Yes, he was. And a father of nine children."

Ella's brows arched. "Wow. And you mentioned spices?"

Massimo nodded and explained that Federico had brought many new spices from India and China to Italy and to his own region of Sardinia, along with other treasures, like the zizibus tree with its olive-sized brown berries.

The Roman emperor had rewarded Federico for his trade initiatives by granting him the title of Baron.

Massimo could see Ella was genuinely interested, her eyes lighting up as he went through the most notable descendants of Federico in the subsequent centuries, including some Robin Hood–like brigands in the 1860s, who ended up becoming folk heroes. When he got to his great-grandfather Alberto, Massimo explained that Alberto's older brother Leonardo—just before the Allied invasion in 1943—had tricked him out of his rightful inheritance and destroyed his reputation, and Alberto ended up dying penniless, his family on the brink of starvation.

"And my grandfather Teodoro, who was twelve when World War II ended, swore he'd find a way to restore the family's good name and fortune.'"

"How did he do that?" Ella leaned forward. "He was just a kid."

"In his day, you were pretty much a young adult at that age. He worked eighteen hours a day for a wealthy landowner, who unlike others who exploited their laborers, rewarded Nonno Teodoro after a few years with a plot of land, some farm animals and a bonus. Teodoro became respected for his honesty and work ethic, and later on, actually became mayor of the village. He eventually discovered documents that revealed Leonardo's dishonesty and corruption, and the law officials restored his title and transferred most of Leonardo's land and holdings to Teodoro.

"My father was Nonno Teodoro's only child and heir. Like our ancestor Federico, he possessed a sharp business sense that eventually led to investments in the resort business. And he taught me everything I know..." He felt his voice unexpectedly cracking with emotion.

"That's really fascinating," Ella said. "You are fortunate to know so much about your family history." She clicked off the recorder and placed it back in her bag along with her notepad. "I wish—" She stopped short. "I'm sorry, it's nothing," she said, averting her gaze.

"Please, finish what you were about to say, Ella. I'm curious about your family history."

Was she actually squirming in her chair? Her cheeks were becoming almost as flushed as ripe persimmons, and she was biting her lower lip. Something was on her mind, something personal...

She eyed him hesitantly, almost as if she were wondering why he would be interested in anything about her. The vulnerability in the depths of her eyes caused his heart muscle to constrict involuntarily, and he realized what he was seeing was evidence of an emotion that he was all too familiar with…*loss*.

Ella set down her notepad and pursed her lips. She inched forward in her armchair, her hands on the armrests, and looked like she wanted more than anything to take flight.

"Ella, *cosa c'è?*" he prompted. "What is bothering you?" He leaned forward and hoped she could see the sincerity in his eyes.

She inhaled deeply and shook her head. "I don't want to bother you with my…personal issues. I'm not here to waste your time."

His eyes narrowed. "It's not a waste of time," he said. "Or a bother. *Prego*."

"I had told you I was adopted," she finally blurted. "But what I didn't tell you was that I was adopted. *Here*. In Sardinia."

CHAPTER NINE

THERE! SHE HAD done it, revealed something about her private life that she hadn't intended to share, least of all with Massimo DiLuca. But something in his eyes had unlocked her trust, and she heard the words spilling out of her mouth before her critical mind could stop her.

"You are… *Sardinian*?" he said huskily.

"Yes. My mother was Canadian, my father Sardinian. My adoptive parents, that is. My birth mother—and presumably my biological father—were Sardinian."

"Were?" His eyes narrowed, like an eagle zooming in on a movement in a field.

"I know nothing about them," she admitted slowly. "My adoptive mother went on a trip to Italy, met my dad in Sardinia. They married, and when she found out she couldn't have children, they decided to adopt. *Me*."

His brow furrowed. "But they didn't stay here? How did you end up in Canada?"

"My father died in a car accident when I was four," she said, swallowing. "My mother returned with me to Canada a few months later." She looked down, staring at her clasped hands. "She passed last year."

"I'm very sorry for your loss, Ella," he said softly. "What were your parents' names?"

"Cassandra and Micheli," she murmured. "Rossi."

"You anglicized your last name to Ross." His eyes bored into her.

His tone was not judgmental, but Ella sensed that he was curious as to why she had changed it.

"It's a long story," she said dismissively. "In a nutshell, I went through a troubled time, struggling with my identity. Struggling with the fact that my biological father took off, refusing to acknowledge his responsibilities, and my birth mother gave me up. I wanted to detach from everything Sardinian, everything Italian. Yes," she answered his unspoken question, "even though my Sardinian father had adopted me. I was so confused…"

He stared at her, his mouth pursed, his hand stroking his beard. "I don't blame you," he said quietly.

The empathy in his voice made her eyes begin to mist up. She squeezed them shut for a moment, determined to stem the tears. "I'm sorry," she said. "I didn't mean to get you involved in my drama." She straightened in her chair, and her handbag, which she had placed over the back of the chair, tipped over, spilling some of the contents.

With a groan of frustration, Ella bent to pick them up off the floor and shoved them back into her handbag. She stood up. The first interview was done, and she was anxious to get back to the guesthouse to review her notes and listen to the recording again.

Massimo stood up and glanced at his watch. "I think this would be a good time for a snack, yes? And something to drink." He frowned. "You look a little pale."

Ella blinked. "Um, sure." She would get to her work after that.

"Andiamo in cucina," he said. *"Cappuccino o bevanda fresca? Aranciata, limonata?"*

"Orange juice is fine," she said, and followed him as he strode through the arched doorway. She could use something cool and fresh. Something that would revitalize her after the emotionally draining episode that had just occurred.

All she wanted to do was forget it. File it away in her mind until the week's interviews were done. Then she could focus on her personal life. Possibly reaching out to her uncle, to start.

As they walked to the kitchen, Ella couldn't help being distracted by the spaciousness and elegance of rooms that flowed into and around each other, connected by a series of incredibly high-arched doorways under vaulted ceilings enhanced by polished wood beams.

Massimo looked back at her as they were walking through the living area and said, "All the larger wood pieces are genuine chestnut and walnut, created by a master carver." Ella nodded, liking the look of the modern furniture: an extra long leather sectional and accent chairs with sleek, carved-wood embellishments, and the intricate, inlaid decorative pieces, like the chessboard on one side table and the main coffee table, which was, Massimo explained, constructed with the technique of geometric marquetry and featured a variety of woods, including cherry and maple.

The furniture's wood finishes contrasted well with the cool white palette of the walls. The main wall featured huge sliding doors leading to an outdoor living space that looked out onto the pool and the sea beyond. Another wall had two alcoves, one with several shelves filled with books, another with decanters and glasses and a concealed wine cooler below.

Massimo pointed out the main wine cellar was in an underground room accessible from the butler's pantry.

Ella was glad that the conversation had shifted from her family history to Massimo's home. She wanted to focus on the reason she was here this week, not the missing pieces of her life... That had to wait until she was finished with the DiLuca family.

She had done interviews in some pretty impressive homes in places like Vancouver and California, but Ella had never seen anything like this villa. If the living room was over the top, the kitchen was even more impressive. The long island, with its gleaming Sardinian stone, spanned the length of the cabinetry.

At Massimo's invitation, she sat on one of the high swivel chairs. She felt as if she were in a soda shop, watching as he took out a juicer and oranges and proceeded to make freshly squeezed juice. He handed her a tall glass and made one for himself, as well.

He remained standing on the other side of the island. When he was halfway through his drink, he set it down and leaned forward to look at her directly. "I'd like to continue our conversation," he said quietly.

"I left my recorder—"

"No, not that conversation." When she didn't reply, he added, "The one about your family."

She waved a hand dismissively. "My mom and dad were wonderful, loving parents. I am happy they chose me. Case closed," she said bluntly.

"Yes, perhaps that part is closed. But you have another part of your history that is not," he said. "Is that why you're staying in Sardinia for a week after our interview sessions are finished? To find some answers about—"

"Well, *maybe*. I'm not sure if my uncle knows anything more than I do." She shifted in the swivel chair. "Thanks for the orange juice. Now if you don't mind, I'd like to head back to start working on the piece."

Massimo said nothing for a moment and then glanced at his watch. "My friend and personal chef is arriving shortly and I will be discussing tonight's dinner menu with him. Is eight o'clock a good time for you?"

"Yes, that's fine. Thank you."

"Foods you dislike?"

"What Italian food could I possibly dislike?" she said, and gave a small chuckle.

He nodded. *"Bellissimo."*

His gaze was direct, his dark eyes gleaming like river stones. "I hope you don't think I was trying to pry, Ella, but I suppose it might have looked that way." He shrugged. "I'm sorry."

She raised a hand. "I'm fine," she said, but it came out sharper than she had intended. "It's just…a sensitive subject. And I don't expect you to understand my situation. Most people can't understand what it's like, either to be adopted or to have to adopt. How can they, unless it happens to them?" She glanced down, feeling a prickle behind her eyelids. "It's just not a topic I like to get into with people who have no idea…"

"…how it feels," he finished for her, his eyes narrowing. "Well, I had no intention of talking about this, Ella, but I do want to set the record straight."

She looked up. He stared over her shoulder for a few seconds. In the distance she heard the thrum of a motorboat. When Massimo gazed back at her, he rubbed at his beard for a moment. "I don't know what it's like to be adopted, Ella, but I know how it feels when your wife can't have children and you both decide that you want to adopt a baby and give her or him your love and the best in life."

She tensed as his words sank in, her heart starting to thump erratically.

As he ran the fingers of one hand through

his hair, her gaze riveted to the muscles tensing along his jaw.

"And I know how it feels when a week later, your wife passes," he ground out the words, his voice a low rumble, "and your dreams of adopting a baby die with her. So even though I didn't actually adopt a child, Ella," he continued, his eyes narrowing, "I can truly imagine how lucky I would have felt—and my wife as well—to have been able to have chosen a baby as our own."

"I—I'm very sorry for your loss," she stammered. "I knew about your wife, but I—"

"You don't have to explain. I didn't want to focus on that in the interview. But we're not doing an interview. This is off the record."

"I'm sorry you weren't able to adopt. I—I know I was lucky to have been chosen and raised by two good people. People who wanted to be parents and who...who loved me," she said, choking on her last words.

"I'm sure they felt lucky too," he murmured, his voice husky. "I wish I had been able to have that opportunity." His gaze bore into hers. "It couldn't have always been easy for you, though."

Ella crossed her arms and sighed. "No, it wasn't always easy. I was teased by some of the kids in my class, who had found out I was adopted. They were mean, saying my birth parents must have been on drugs or that I must have been ugly when I was born and my parents couldn't stand to look at me so they gave me away." She bit her lip. "Kids can be so cruel. Because I was 'different,' I was often last to be picked when there were teams to be chosen. Or not invited to some birthday parties." She paused, frowning. It was amazing these past injuries still had the power to cause her pain.

"That must have felt hurtful."

"And lonely." She nodded. "I kept it from my parents, not wanting them to feel hurt, too."

"You were a sensitive little girl."

The empathy in his voice made her swallow. If she didn't leave soon, she'd be awash in tears.

Ella was blinking at him, her forehead creased, looking like she was on the verge of tears. He hadn't wanted to upset her; he had just wanted her to know that his earlier words weren't shallow. His stomach had twisted when she had first revealed her mother had given her up for adoption, and at that time, he couldn't bring himself to formulate the appropriate words to show his empathy.

What could he have possibly said? "I'm

sorry your mother gave you up for adoption?" Especially since he and Rita had hoped for a mother to do just that...

He swallowed, feeling as if there was a wedge of grief blocking his esophagus. Those memories were still raw at times.

They had talked about the possibility of adopting after discovering that she couldn't conceive. Rita had looked at him with a twinkle in her eye, and said she'd be happy with either a boy or girl, but that there were so many adorable baby clothes out there for girls. And a week later, she was gone, along with all their dreams for the future.

Ella opened her mouth to say something, but the drone of the motorboat drowned out her words. They both turned and saw it approaching the dock, and a few moments later, the rumble subsided.

"That would be Chef Angelo," he said. "He has two Michelin stars to his credit, and he loves cooking so much he accepted my request for him to come to *Villa Serena* several times a week to prepare a feast. Afterward, he hurries off to his seaside restaurant in Cagliari, the *Mare e Cielo*, which is all you see when you're there, as it sits on top of a hill. Why don't I introduce you before you go back to the guesthouse?"

Ella shook her head quickly. "Thanks, but I have a slight headache. Please pass on my regrets."

"You will still join me for dinner?"

"If this headache doesn't linger, perhaps," she said. "And about what you said before." She pursed her lips. "I'm sorry if I—"

He put up a hand. "Please. Don't worry. I understand."

He accompanied Ella to his office to retrieve her handbag, and then they proceeded to the foyer and he opened the door for her. She nodded and said "ciao" before continuing on toward the guesthouse.

Massimo turned and waved to the man who was not only a celebrated chef in Sardinia, recognized also on the mainland and in Europe, but a good friend too. They had been each other's best man, and had often gone to social events together with their wives. Angelo had been there for him during the rockiest time of his life: the year after Rita had passed.

Massimo greeted Angelo with a hug. Angelo was like a brother to him.

"What would *signorina* Ross like tonight?" He raised an eyebrow at Massimo.

"She's not fussy. See what you can find and work your magic, Angelo."

Angelo went to gather fresh herbs from the

courtyard garden outside the kitchen, and Massimo went up to his room. He wanted a few moments to himself to process everything that had just occurred between him and Ella.

He opened up the balcony doors and stood at the ornate railing, watching the foamy surf creep up to the beach and leave a scalloped design that reminded him of the lacy edge of a wedding gown. And then the design dissipated as the waves broke and receded back into the sea. Massimo filled his lungs with the fresh sea air and exhaled slowly.

The atmosphere on *Villa Serena* had changed, he realized. For better or worse, that was something he had yet to determine. He did know one thing: somehow, discovering that Ella was born in Sardinia brought a whole new dimension to the situation. What were the chances of a journalist from a New York City magazine actually being Sardinian? Sardinian-Canadian now...

Massimo hadn't planned on revealing any details about his personal life to her. He talked to very few people about his late wife; his circle of trust included predominantly a grief counselor, his mother and Angelo. But when Ella was implying that he didn't understand anything about being adopted or wanting to adopt, he had instinctively wanted to explain.

And surprisingly, his words had come out fairly easily compared to how difficult it had been in the first months and year to even say the word *died* or even *passed*. And he hadn't even shared the part about his wife's infertility and their decision to look into the adoption process to his mother or Angelo. He had discussed that aspect of his grief with only his counselor.

From his balcony, Massimo could also look across at the guest villa and the balcony of the room where Ella would be sleeping. He thought about where they had left off when Angelo arrived and wished that they had been able to continue the conversation.

Ella hadn't seemed too willing to talk about her plans to stay in Sardinia once their interview sessions were over. She had been very abrupt, changing the subject immediately. It was obviously a sensitive subject, and one she had been planning to deal with completely on her own.

Not that he had any notion of butting into her affairs when it came to exploring her family history.

But he *had* wanted to ask her where she would be staying for the week after the interviews.

He shook his head. Why was he trying to

solve her problems? If she hadn't already booked a place, why should he even worry about it? Ella Ross… *Rossi*…was an adult, quite capable of looking after herself.

"Ella Rossi," he murmured, liking the way her Italian name sounded. He took one last glance at his guesthouse and went back downstairs. On the way to the kitchen, he passed his office, where a bright flash on the floor by his desk caught his eye. He walked in and reached for it, his eyebrows lifting when he saw that it was the gold lettering on the cover of a passport.

He would give it to Ella when she came for dinner. He strode over to the sideboard and deposited it into one of the drawers before heading to the kitchen to see where Angelo was at with the preparation of his courses.

CHAPTER TEN

As soon as she returned to the guesthouse, Ella set down her notepad and recorder by her laptop on the desk in the study and returned to the kitchen for water to take with a tablet. She would look over her notes and listen to the recording once her headache had subsided.

She plopped onto one of the recliners with a view of the cove. The adrenalin was still pumping through her since Massimo had dropped the bombshell about his and his wife's plans to adopt.

She hadn't been able to face meeting his chef after that, and she had made her way quickly to the guesthouse, her mind a jumble of thoughts and questions.

Whatever Ella had been expecting Massimo to say after her blunt comment about people not having any idea when it came to adoption issues, it hadn't been *that*. It added a new layer to her understanding of what he had gone through, as if losing his wife hadn't been enough.

Ella's mother had often shared with her how happy and excited she and Micheli had been, knowing that they would be able to adopt. And how they had been even more delighted the first time they saw her two days after she was born. She hadn't been given a name, and when Cassandra had taken her in her arms, she had looked out the window at the sea and then, misty-eyed, had said to Micheli, who had had his arms around her, that she wanted to call the baby Marinella, the diminutive form of *marina*, a name of Latin origin meaning "of the sea."

"She's our little Sardinian miracle," Micheli had replied, bending to kiss the baby gently on the forehead. *"Benedica."*

Ella blinked back tears. Every time her mother had recounted the story, Ella had become emotional. Especially at her father's whispered blessing.

And now, to know that Massimo had been robbed of the opportunity to know the joy of adopting, and to imagine how devastating it had been for him to lose his wife and their shared dreams, was overwhelming.

He had lost a partner, just as her mother had lost hers. Ella had been only four at the time, but she could still vaguely remember her mother's sadness, her crying. Her mother's tight hugs when Ella had asked, *"Quando ritorna a casa papà?"*

She had wanted to know when her father was coming back home even after they had moved to Canada. When Ella was older, her mother told her that she had been sad too, crying for her *papà*, especially at night, missing story time and his bedtime blessing. Her mother would reply with the same story about heaven, the stars and angel wings, and him being close by...

Ella had been comforted by her mother's words as she had tucked her in, her mother's whispered *"Buona notte, Marinella,"* the last thing she heard before falling asleep.

Ella swallowed. Her mother had continued to call her Marinella after she had decided to change her name. And Ella hadn't actually gone so far as to formally change it. Her mother had also continued to speak to her in Italian regularly so she wouldn't forget her first language, which Cassandra had studied in high school and university before taking a trip to Italy when she had graduated.

Ella's thoughts flew back to the man she would be in close contact with for the week ahead. She had made a mistaken judgment about him, and she hoped that the air had been cleared between them. She would get a feel for the situation at dinner tonight...

It would be hours before dinner, though. The headache tablet had started to kick in, and Ella decided to return to the study. She would work on the piece for a good stretch and then take some time later in the afternoon to walk along the beach, and maybe even go for a swim in the cove.

Satisfied with what she had accomplished, Ella shut down her laptop and strode to the kitchen.

She peered at the contents of the pantry and the fridge, and decided to make a fruit salad with a little honey and lemon juice. She left it on the island while she went to the bedroom to change into a bathing suit and a loose top and shorts. She applied some sunscreen to her face, arms and legs, stuffed a hat and towel into a beach bag, and put on a pair of canvas flats and sunglasses before returning to the kitchen for her fruit salad.

She took it out with her and walked down to the cove. Sitting on the chaise lounge where Massimo had almost spent the night, she enjoyed her sweet snack while watching the surf tumble onto the shore in a frothy explosion and recede with a gentle swoosh back into the translucent turquoise waters. The late afternoon sun felt wonderful on her face and she tilted it to the sky, breathing in the salt-tinged air contentedly.

Feeling like a pampered cat stretched out on a patch of soft grass, Ella breathed in and out slowly, thinking what a great place this would be to do an outdoor yoga routine in the morning. Or even later in the day. She set down her empty bowl on a side table and decided to walk along the beach and return when she was good and hot, ready to be refreshed in the sea. She put on her hat and set off, marveling at the fact that she had the island practically all to herself.

She pictured Massimo walking along the beach before diving into the crystal-clear waters and emerging moments later, his muscled shoulders and arms glistening with the jeweled drops of sunlit water.

And then she berated herself silently for having such wayward thoughts, only to have a rebounding one: she was human and Massimo was a gorgeous man that many woman would want to—

No. Stop thinking. Keep walking.

Ella scanned the beach for shells and collected ones with unique colors or shapes and put them into her shorts' pockets. It was a perfect summer day, the sun hot but not scorching, with the sea breeze fanning her cheeks.

The only sounds she heard were the cries of seagulls and other unfamiliar birds and the surf. She tried to imagine what it was like actually living on the island... Massimo must have found it to be healing, with the lush vegetation, and the sea with its soothing murmur always around him.

After about a half hour or so, Ella heard the thrum of a motor. Angelo must have finished whipping up dinner for the evening and was heading back to his restaurant. She checked the time on her watch and saw that she had time for a quick swim before getting ready to go to *Villa Serena* for the meal.

By the time she arrived at the cove, Ella was more than ready to cool off. She slipped out of her top and shorts, flung them on the chaise lounge along with her hat and watch, and after removing her canvas flats, she walked gingerly into the lapping waters. The surf met her with a foamy rush, making her catch her breath. She dove in and came up refreshed and exhilarated. She swam for a bit and then floated, letting her muscles relax completely as she looked up at the baby blue sky.

A sensation of pure delight filled her, and she wanted to simultaneously shout out her joy and cry. The last time she had splashed in Sardinian waters was with her parents when she was four. And now she was back, twenty-four years later. Ella made an instant decision to save her tears of nostalgia for another time. Her mother and *papà* would want her to be happy now, not sad.

With a sudden feeling of freedom, Ella let out a whoop and as she treaded water, she slapped at the waves playfully and eventually allowed the surf to push her toward the shore.

She emerged from the sea with a light heart, but when she squeezed her eyes to clear her vision, she froze.

She wasn't alone.

Massimo was striding through the oleander path toward her. Had he seen her splashing about in the water? He must have. She shivered as a slight breeze swept past and, eyeing the large towel she had left on the chaise lounge, realized in dismay that the baron would reach her before she could walk over and grab the towel. And it would look pretty foolish if she made a dash for it.

Sensing the sweep of his dark eyes over her even from a distance, Ella self-consciously crossed her arms, certain her face was lobster red if the sizzle under her skin was any indication.

Massimo had texted Ella that Angelo had left and, if her headache had subsided, she could join him for a pre-dinner drink, but she hadn't responded. He had gone down to knock at the guesthouse door. When she hadn't answered, he'd figured she'd gone for a walk, and a quick check of the cove had confirmed this, as he could see the direction of her footprints.

He had gone back to the villa, but when she still hadn't returned after forty-five minutes, he had begun to worry. He had headed to the cove and caught sight of her in the sea, her arms flapping wildly. He had felt a jolt in his chest, and his adrenalin had kicked in, priming his body to leap in to save her. And then she had swiveled around and it had been clear that she was having fun. He had taken a few deep breaths to calm his pulsing heartbeat before continuing on toward her.

When Ella had emerged from the water, her tangerine one-piece swimsuit clinging to her and rivulets from her dark hair dripping over her, he had experienced another jolt.

It was just the surprise of seeing another person in the water, on his beach, nothing more.

A person by the enchanting name of Marinella.

Massimo had felt his pulse spike as the words of "Marina," an older but popular Italian song came to him, about a man falling in love with a brunette called Marina, but she didn't want to hear about it, and the man wondered what he should do to conquer her heart.

At that moment, Ella had caught sight of him and stopped in her tracks. Massimo could see his presence had jolted her, as well, and not wanting to make her uncomfortable, he had stayed where he was.

"*Ciao*, Ella." He waved. "I texted, but there was no answer. I had come to see if you were feeling better and if you wanted to join me for a pre-dinner drink."

"Yes, I'm feeling much better. I—I'll just need a few minutes to change and then I'll join you."

Massimo turned and made his way back to the villa, unable to make the image of Ella splashing about in the sparkling waters disappear from his mind.

In the dining room, Massimo poured himself a glass of Prosecco and surveyed the table he had set for the two of them. It had been so strange, laying out a second place-setting for someone other than his mother. And he had had to think about where exactly to position Ella. He couldn't possibly have her sitting at the opposite end of the table, which would have been ridiculously too far away. He finally decided that he would change his own place setting from the head of the table to the next seat, and Ella's would be directly opposite him.

Massimo sauntered into the living area and set down his glass on the coffee table before sitting on one of the reclining armchairs facing the opened retractable-glass walls. He felt a slight tension in his stomach muscles and wondered if it had been caused by his concern over Ella or if it was because he was about to have dinner with a guest. *A woman.* And the first visitor to stay on his island.

It was purely business. And practical, since she was here for the week. They would enjoy Angelo's four-course dinner and then she would return to the guesthouse and he would...

What would he do?

Ordinarily, he was alone in the evening, which was pretty well always unless Angelo had time to linger or stay for the meal. Which was rare, since he was running an acclaimed restaurant that his guests frequented not only for the Michelin-rated food but for Angelo's lively presence.

And if Massimo's mother came for a visit, it would usually be for an early-afternoon lunch. So Massimo spent evenings walking along the beach, swimming either in the sea or his pool, reading, writing down ideas and making rough sketches to enhance his resort business, watching a documentary or classic film, and occasionally trying out a new Sardinian recipe.

Tonight…he shrugged. He would see…

He reached for his glass and let a swirl of the Prosecco tingle his taste buds. Angelo had prepared a platter of *salati*, tasty appetizers that he would take out when Ella arrived.

After Angelo had gone, Massimo had changed into a teal shirt and light gray trousers. Belt but no tie. That would have been too formal. He had assessed his image in the full-length mirror in his dressing room and had thought *still too formal*. He had then folded the sleeves up to below his elbows. Satisfied, he had headed downstairs and had texted Ella, and then had made his way to the guesthouse to see if she was there.

At the sound of footsteps outside, he quickly rose and went around to the front entrance. Ella was approaching with a tentative smile on her face. Her short-sleeved turquoise peasant dress made her look so…young and carefree. She was carrying a gift bag, and when she was at the entrance, she handed it to him. "A little something from Canada," she said, "to thank you for your generosity in allowing me to stay in your guesthouse."

"That wasn't necessary…but thank you." He

held the door open for her. "*Prego.* Come and have some Prosecco and appetizers while I open this," he said, setting the bag on his armchair.

As she sipped her drink, he reached into the gift bag and extracted a bottle of Niagara ice wine, a maple-leaf-shaped bottle of Ontario maple syrup, and an official Toronto Maple Leafs cap. He nodded appreciatively. "*Grazie,* Ella. That was very kind."

"I also wanted to apologize for making assumptions about you earlier," she said. "That wasn't so kind."

His eyes narrowed. "So we're even, then."

"Wh-what do you mean?" she said, her brow creasing.

"I had made assumptions about you. About your age and experience…" He raised his eyebrows. "So are we good, then?" he asked with a chuckle. "No more fighting?"

Ella's eyes widened. "You haven't seen fighting, *signor* DiLuca." She had another drink of her *aperitivo.* "And remember, I hold the coveted Moorish sword in my castle. Woe to the foolish one who tests my patience."

Massimo laughed. "I'm making a new assumption…that I now hold the title of Foolish One and not Baron."

She tilted her chin up then nodded solemnly. "Correct."

He smiled, and picked up their empty Prosecco glasses. "I think we'd better get started with dinner."

"May I help?" she said, following him into the dining room.

"Yes," he said, "you can help by starting with some appetizers." He set the platter on the table and pulled her chair out. She sat down and he pointed to the selection that Ella was eyeing with interest. Chickpeas with fennel, olive-oil-and-lemon-drizzled octopus salad, spiced olives, and a variety of cheeses and crostini. She helped herself to a small portion of each.

"I want to find a good Sardinian cookbook while I'm here," Ella said, in between bites.

"Your mother—?"

"Was Canadian, as I had mentioned," Ella said. "She learned a few recipes from my father's mother—like *sebadas*—and once we moved back to Canada, she made them once in a while, knowing how much I loved them."

They ate the first course, an artichoke-heart soup, in companionable silence for a few minutes. Massimo hadn't been sure how he would feel, sharing a meal with a woman after the past few years... He stole several glances at Ella, pleased that she was enjoying it.

Angelo had timed things perfectly, Massimo thought, leaving to get the pork stew with fava beans that had been simmering for a couple of hours in the oven.

"So you want to reacquaint yourself with your Sardinian heritage?" he said, pouring a ladleful of the stew onto each of their plates. He passed her a bowl filled with thick slices of *civraxiu*, a hearty dipping bread.

"Yes, which is why I'm staying for a week after our interviews." Her eyes widened. "Oh, my gosh. I was supposed to look into booking a place." She set down her fork. "I must do that right after dinner."

"I can help you," he said. "I have contacts all over. But first, let's enjoy this and Angelo's homemade cookies with an espresso, and then we can find you a place."

He poured them each a glass of strong red wine, a *Cannonau di Sardegna* from one of his own vineyards. *"Salute,"* he said, raising his glass toward her in a toast.

"Salute," she replied. She inhaled the bouquet and swirled it around before tasting it. "Very nice." She smiled. "It tastes like… Sardinia."

He laughed and gestured at her stew. "Enjoy this other taste of Sardinia."

He watched as she took her first bite.

"It's delicious. Please thank Angelo for me."

He took out his cell phone and sent Angelo a quick text.

Done!

At the end of the course, Ella sat back with a sigh. "Everything has been delicious. *Grazie*, Massimo." She gave him a warm smile, and the genuine appreciation in her eyes caused a quickening in his chest.

He had craved solitude after his wife passed, and except for the times when Angelo or his mother came by, he had spent the bulk of the last three years in solitude on his island. Now, having shared a pleasant hour dining with Ella, an inner voice suggested that perhaps he was ready to start making some changes in his life...and entertain the thought of letting more people...or maybe another woman...in his world.

Their gazes connected several times over the fruit course and later as they were drinking their espressos, and Massimo didn't know whether he should be happy about the effect she was having on him physically or if he should be heeding the alarm signal in his head.

Massimo swallowed his espresso and set down his cup.

"Scusami," he said. He reached over to open the drawer of the sideboard and withdrew her passport. "I'm sure you don't want to lose it.

You had dropped it on the floor of my study, and it ended up under my desk."

Ella raised her eyebrows. "No, I don't want to lose that." She leaned across the table to take it from him. "Although I wouldn't mind losing the photo," she said with a chuckle, opening up the booklet. "I look pretty grim, since they want you to refrain from smiling."

"I can't imagine you looking grim," he said, his mouth quirking.

She smirked and held up the photo for him to see.

He smiled at her almost stern expression and then his gaze shifted to the information on the right-hand side of the photo.

Something clanged against his ribs when he read the name.

Not Ella Ross or Ella Rossi, but Marinella Rossi.

"Marinella," he murmured, and gazed at her in wonder.

She started, and setting the passport down on the table, she gazed at Massimo wordlessly for a moment.

"Would you like me to continue to call you Ella or should I address you as Marinella?"

"Um, well, I…either one works, although my mother and father's family were the only ones who called me Marinella. The other people who have called me that—like at the airport back home—always pronounced it like the first part of *marinate*. I do prefer Marinella pronounced the Italian way."

"I wouldn't be pronouncing it any other way," he said with a soft laugh. "Just as I like the fact that you pronounce my name the Italian way, and not 'Mass-im-o.'"

Her cheeks had blushed to a deep pink, and averting her gaze to check the time, she said, "How about I help you with these dishes, and then I can look for a place to stay…?"

"How about you don't and we head directly to my office computer? I'm sure you're anxious to find a place before they all get booked up, which is not unusual at this time of year."

"Va bene." She nodded. "If you're sure."

He stared at her wordlessly for a moment, distracted by the way her dark eyes looked like glistening chestnuts after a downpour. *"Sì, Marinella,"* he said finally. "I'm sure."

CHAPTER ELEVEN

"You never told me where your father was from," Massimo said as he sat down at his desk. He had pulled up a chair for Ella right next to him. "And if there are any relatives still there."

"He was from the medieval village of Posada. My *nonna* and *nonno* had only two sons, my father and his brother, Domenicu. They had a farm on the outskirts, not on the hillside itself, and they lived off the land. *Zio* Domenicu would be the sole living relative left, unless he married and had children." She inhaled and exhaled deeply. "And I know nothing about my birth parents, except that my mother was young when she had me, and my biological father apparently denied any responsibility. He took off, moving to the mainland, and my mother never revealed his identity." Ella fell silent as old emotions churned inside her.

As a child, she had created so many possible

scenarios: her mother really wanted to keep her, but her parents forced her to give her up because they couldn't afford to feed one more person; her mother's rich parents had sent her away for nine months to keep it a secret from their rich friends and would have nothing to do with a child whose father's identity was unknown. And on and on.

Ella wanted to believe that her mother had wanted her, but being under age, she had no choice but to consent to the will of her parents. Her biological grandparents had become the villains in Ella's eyes when her adoptive mother had revealed to her about her birth mother being so young.

Massimo let out a heavy sigh. "I can't even imagine how difficult all this must have been for you. Wondering why your biological parents…"

Ella felt the back of her eyes start to prickle at his words. "It does something to you, you know, makes you question your identity, your worth, even." Her eyes blurred and she shut them tight, pressing against them with the heels of her hands. "Sorry," she said. "I don't want to ruin the evening."

Ella felt Massimo's hands over hers. She felt her body tense up. He brought her hands down and reached into his pocket. "New handkerchief," he said huskily. "Never used…and no, you're not ruining the evening." He dabbed gently at her eyes and when he was done, she opened them, and for a long moment, their gazes locked.

He moved back. Rubbing his temple, he said, "You're not used to the Sardinian sun, Ella, and you were out for quite a while today. You're probably more tired than you think…so why don't we look at this tomorrow morning? Don't worry, we'll find you a place."

Ella nodded. Yes, she was tired. Physically and emotionally. She did not decline his offer to walk her down to the guesthouse. It was dark with few stars tonight, and she didn't want to meet any night creatures, winged or otherwise.

When they got to the main doors, she thanked Massimo for the exceptional dinner and for accompanying her.

"Prego." He nodded, a corner of his mouth tilting upward. *"Buona notte, Marinella."* He opened the door for her. *"Sogni d'oro."*

Massimo sprinted back up to his villa, sure that the drumming he was hearing was originating in his chest and not the forested part of the island.

He'd wanted to kiss her.

Thank God he hadn't.

She would be here for four more days, and the last thing he desired was to complicate things.

Before that moment occurred, he had just wanted to hold Ella's hands, wipe her tears. But when she had opened her eyes, he had caught a glimpse of her Sardinian sensitivity and strength...and he had been overcome with a desire to immerse himself in those depths. The first time he had felt any such desire for so long...

Massimo tossed his shirt on a chair and strode to his balcony. Looking up through his telescope at the stars or moon always relaxed him. Tonight the moon was especially luminous, and he watched it for several minutes. The night breeze was cool, but he welcomed its feathery strokes over his heated body. Looking over the moonlit crowns of the oleander trees in the distance to the only room of the guesthouse that was lit, and where Ella would be getting ready for bed, Massimo's heart clanged with a sudden realization.

He was alive.

Massimo woke up during the night, and as he stared at the open doors of his balcony, the details of the previous evening came flooding back.

How Ella had enjoyed the Sardinian feast Angelo had prepared. The brief teasing exchange between them. And how Ella had shared more of her personal feelings about being adopted… It had bothered him earlier to hear kids had been mean to her, and he thought now how sad he'd be if he knew that his adopted child was being teased or bullied.

He fell back into a troubled sleep, and when he woke up again, the east window revealed a sky streaked with bands of orange and gold as the sun emerged from the horizon. It was earlier than usual for his morning jog, but his brain was too busy for him to stay in bed.

In minutes he was dressed in his jogging clothes and was out the door and on the beach. One of the reasons he had fallen in love with this island, other than for the solitude, was because of its impossibly long beach and enchanting cove. His real estate agent had arranged for a few flights around Sardinia, and Massimo had spotted the diamond-shaped island with the pretty white rim that turned out to be a sparkling strip of pristine shore.

He never regretted the decision to build *Villa Serena* on this idyllic island. While he lived in the guesthouse, and even after he moved into the villa, he spent as much time outdoors as inside. He enjoyed his early morning jog, and he often ended the day with an evening stroll.

Massimo checked the time on his watch before starting his job. By the time he was done, he'd still have plenty of time for a shower and an espresso before Ella arrived. In fact, he'd have time to call his mother, also, and confirm the details for dinner at her villa.

What would his mother think of Ella? Massimo's instinct told him she would approve. There was no pretentiousness about Ella, unlike some of the daughters of his mother's friends. And he wasn't so naive as to believe that his mother had wanted to have this party for her sixty-fifth birthday for her benefit alone. No, his *mamma* was *furba*, a sly one, wanting to nudge him in the direction of eligible women.

He shook his head. He would indulge his mother with a birthday to remember, but as much as she wanted him to see him settled, it would happen on his own terms, and when he was ready.

Massimo slowed down and then jogged on the spot while reaching for his water bottle. The sun, looking like a shiny persimmon against a sky tinged with splashes of apricot and pink, was reflected in the sea. He stopped and took it all in, never tiring of the views.

It had been a balm from the very beginning, when he was still reeling from the blow of his wife's passing, a reminder that beauty existed alongside the dark moments in life.

He recalled another such moment during his first night in the finished guesthouse. He had been walking around the exterior of the property, pleased with the landscaping, but he had suddenly experienced a stab of loneliness, knowing that it was for his eyes only. His gaze had riveted on the wildflower accent garden and a Corsican swallowtail butterfly that had fluttered into view and settled onto a plant. It had stunning yellow-and-black markings on wings that were intermittently opening and closing, and small blue spots edged the hind wings, along with two red spots. Massimo had watched, transfixed, struck by the ability to experience sadness and pleasure simultaneously.

And then it had fluttered away, making him think of how Rita had been in his life for a short period and was gone...

Every time he had seen a swallowtail butterfly after that, Massimo had felt, foolish or not, as if it were a sign Rita was at peace, and he had been comforted.

Massimo jogged back to his villa and had a refreshing shower. It was still early, but he could tell that it was going to be a scorcher of a day. The timed sprinkler system had begun to water the gardens, and as he prepared his espresso, he contemplated going for a swim in his pool once the interview with Ella was over.

After finishing his espresso, Massimo worked in his study, reviewing the weekly reports that his resort managers sent him. Afterward, he checked the progress of his latest resort, still in the construction stage and as yet unnamed. It was located in the Maddalena Archipelago, with an enchanting pink beach and mesmerizing views of translucent waters ranging from cerulean to turquoise. Perhaps he'd fly out there after his mother's birthday and the opening of the DiLuca Cardiac Research Center. Maybe it was time to start coming out of his self-imposed seclusion and go back to surveying the progress of his resorts in person.

Maybe he should loosen up in other ways, too.

He reached for his cell phone. There was no reason why he couldn't invite Ella to join him for a swim after the interview session. It wasn't as if he were breaching—or intended to breach—any professional protocols. He had a huge pool meant to be used, and perhaps Ella would appreciate the offer. Why shouldn't he demonstrate his hospitality in this way?

He sent a text before he could change his mind.

Her response came a minute later.

Sure.

And then another one a few seconds after that.

As long as I'm not in deep water, lol.

Massimo stared at the screen. A coil of electricity surged through his veins at the fact that Ella was comfortable enough to tease him...

If anyone was in deep water, it was *him*.

CHAPTER TWELVE

AFTER FINISHING HER cappuccino and hazelnut biscotti, Ella went up to the bedroom loft and slipped on a canary yellow swimsuit with white polka dots and straps that tied around her neck, retro-style. She chose a white short-sleeved shirt and a navy wrap-around skirt to wear over the top of the suit for the interview.

As she dressed, she was aware of a fluttering in her stomach. Inviting her for dinner was one thing. It was just being hospitable. But she had never expected the baron to invite her to spend any *personal* time with him. And swimming in his pool was definitely personal. But obviously it was something he did with people staying in his guesthouse.

And then she remembered that she was the first person to stay in his guesthouse.

She thought about what she had impulsively texted back to him. She had instantly regretted taking such a familiar tone with him, but a few moments later, he had responded with a laugh emoji, and she had sighed in relief.

And she also had to ignore the sensation she had felt last night when he had gently wiped her tears and when, seconds later, she couldn't look away from the startling intensity in his eyes.

She had gone to bed with a hundred contradictory thoughts in her head. Thoughts that told her she was living in a world of fantasy, thinking Baron Massimo DiLuca was actually attracted to her. That the Sardinian wine she had enjoyed with her dinner was causing her head to swirl with these ridiculous notions... like the one of him wanting to kiss her...

Shaking her head dismissively, Ella grabbed her bag with her recorder, notepad and personal items, and after slipping into a pair of flip-flops, headed to *Villa Serena*.

She breathed in the sultry morning air, heavy with humidity. By the time she reached Massimo's villa, she felt a sheen on her face and forehead, and she quickly pulled a tissue from her bag. A swim would be a welcome relief after the interview.

Instead of sitting in his office, Massimo suggested doing the interview in the living room, where they could be more relaxed. He carried in two tall glasses of lemonade and motioned for Ella to sit on an armchair by one accent table, and he moved to one edge of the sectional nearest her.

"Tell me about your father," she said, after turning on the recorder.

Massimo stared at Ella for a few seconds.

"You had mentioned your father was your *nonno* Teodoro's only child and heir and that he had a sharp business sense that eventually led him to make some good investments," she prompted, looking up from her notes. "And earlier, you had said *Villa Paradiso* was your family's first resort…"

He nodded. "*Papà* bought it when it was a small, run-down hotel called the *Albergo al Mare*, the Hotel by the Sea. He saw the potential in the vast property it came with. He had the building torn down, and he worked on new designs with an architect friend, then called in any and all of his friends in the construction business to help in his venture. *Papà* was savvy, even in the pre-computer era, and wasn't afraid to take risks."

Massimo shifted his gaze to the sea, where whitecaps were popping up and down in the distance. His voice had softened, and Ella could hear in his tone the admiration and respect he had for his father. "*Papà* accessed all the advertising avenues he could find, and it wasn't long before tourists were flooding to *Villa Paradiso*," he continued, gazing back at Ella. "Of course it has been renovated over the years to reflect the times and the particular tastes of our clients."

"Luxurious tastes," Ella murmured. "And tell me more about how your father 'taught you everything you know.'"

Massimo talked about his father's work ethic and his devotion to his family. "He worked hard, but he always made sure to kick a soccer ball around with me when he came home…"

He swallowed, and Ella felt a twinge in her heart.

"And he often took me on site to show me the construction progress. I was always struck by the way he treated everyone who worked on the project, from the architect to the cleaning staff. He was a good man," he said, his lips pursing as he looked away.

Ella stopped herself from saying "and so are you…" She decided to divert her line of questioning to the matriarch of the family. "Has your mother influenced you in any way?"

Massimo looked at her and laughed. "*Mamma* influences everybody she is with. You will experience the phenomenon that is my mother tonight."

Ella listened to Massimo explaining what

a doting mother she had been throughout his childhood and adolescence, and what a dynamic business partner she had been with his father. And still was with him. He suddenly stopped when his phone buzzed. "Speak of the devil." He laughed, winking at Ella.

Ella turned off the recorder. She was glad he was distracted and couldn't see her cheeks. She had several sips of her lemonade and couldn't help listening to Massimo's side of the conversation. She liked the way he sounded when he spoke Italian…in his deep voice, with its husky notes. She closed her eyes and just listened to the melody of it and not the words themselves. Suddenly it changed, and she realized he had transitioned to Sardinian. And then back to Italian before saying *arrivederci*.

Massimo's obviously tight relationship with his mother made Ella's loss of her own feel even greater. Her chest felt weighted down with sudden grief. What the baron and *baronessa* shared was the closeness that she had had with her adoptive mother. God, she missed her…

Ella squeezed her eyes tightly. She had to get control of herself before—

"Stai bene, Ella?" Massimo said.

Her eyes flew open. He was leaning forward and staring directly at her.

"Yes, I'm fine," she blurted. How long had he watched her like that? She peered at her notes and continued with her questions about the early years and how the DiLuca resorts had become renowned as elite holiday destinations. And how they had chosen the particular locations for their resorts.

When the two-hour segment was done, Massimo rose from the sectional and said, "Snack or swim?"

"I'd rather have a swim first, thanks." Ella put away her recorder and notepad and looked at him. "Where shall I—?"

"There's an outdoor change area," he said. You'll see it as soon as you step out into the lounge. I'll be there shortly. I'll change upstairs."

Moments later Ella walked into the spacious room that included several changing cubicles and an open, turquoise-tiled section in one corner for pre-swim showers. She removed her blouse and skirt and hung them on the hooks inside her cubicle. After fixing her hair in a ponytail and showering quickly, she proceeded to the infinity pool.

The water temperature was perfect. Ella walked down the pool steps and waded farther in. She immersed herself up to her neck, and when she bobbed up again, she caught a glimpse of Massimo entering the change room. Her heartbeat quickened. She began to swim toward the infinity edge, her adrenalin surging at the thought that any minute, the billionaire baron would be in the pool with her.

It just seemed so unreal.

She was treading water just as Massimo emerged from the shower. Ella was relieved he was wearing swim shorts and not the briefs that many Italian men seemed to prefer when at the beach. It was hard enough not staring at his muscular torso and legs as he walked, without having to focus on anything more... more defined.

From the opposite end of the pool, Massimo waved and dove in. He emerged halfway across the pool, shook his head and then began to swim toward her. Ella's heart pounded. It was one thing to be sitting across from Massimo DiLuca during an interview; it was quite another to watch him do a powerful breast-stroke toward her.

"Bello, no?" he said, now treading water only a few feet away.

Ella knew that he was referring to either the pool or the view or to the act of swimming in such a gorgeous location, and she quickly replied, *"Bellissimo."*

"You're welcome to use the pool anytime

while you are here," he said. And then he grinned. *"Facciamo una gara, Marinella?"*

"Uh, assolutamente...no!" She laughed. "I'm not prepared to race someone who gets to practice in a place like this for much of the year."

"Dai, come on, it's just for fun."

Ella couldn't believe what she was hearing. Massimo DiLuca, the reclusive baron, trying to convince her to have a friendly race.

"Va bene," she capitulated. "But you're taller than me, which will give you the advantage."

He chuckled. "You can start a few seconds before me."

She nodded. "Game on!"

Massimo was surprised at himself for suggesting a race and even more surprised Ella had agreed. It had been a long time since he had felt the desire to be playful, and now that he had blurted the proposition to Ella, he couldn't very well change his mind.

"Freestyle?" he said.

"Freestyle." She nodded.

He got out of the pool and walked to the deep end. Ella followed and as she proceeded to join him, Massimo felt his pulse quicken. Ella looked so picture perfect in that yellow swimsuit. It had a simple style, like something out of a 1950s film, and its mix of innocence and charm really suited her. And what he liked about the way Ella moved was that she wasn't walking as if she were on a catwalk displaying the latest fashions. She wasn't trying to impress anyone.

Yes, he liked that. He liked *real*.

When they were both standing outside the edge of the pool, Massimo nodded. *"Sei pronta?"*

"Yes, I'm ready," she said, shifting from one foot to another.

"Allora… You can start!"

Massimo watched Ella dive in, waited five seconds, then dove in, also. He caught up easily to Ella and they swam side by side for several yards. Their hands brushed into each other, and as Massimo lifted and turned his head, he saw a fleeting glimpse of her focused expression.

It made him smile…and splutter as the pool water immediately found its way into his mouth and down his windpipe. It broke his stride, and he began to tread water as he coughed and cleared his throat.

He looked ahead and saw Ella raise her arm up triumphantly as she reached the other side. When she turned to see where he was at, she put her hand up to her mouth, her eyes crinkling. He smirked and gave a shrug before resuming the front crawl toward her.

"I didn't realize you were so competitive," he said, his mouth twitching as he reached the edge of the pool.

"I didn't know you liked to drink pool water," she retorted, laughing.

He chuckled, shaking his head. "Swim or snack?"

"Snack. My win has made me ravenous."

Massimo stroked his beard. "I think the winner should treat the second-place winner."

"To…?"

"Whatever you think is a treat," he said with a mischievous gleam in his eyes.

"Hmm. I'm not in the habit of treating men, and I'm not sure if what I consider a treat for myself would be appreciated by a man."

"And what exactly would you consider a treat for you—or women in general?"

"A bubble bath. A visit to a bookstore. A night out at a fancy restaurant. Curling up in my pajamas to watch a classic film with a bowl of popcorn. *Or ice cream.* A nice mass—" Ella stopped abruptly and just blinked at him.

Massimo smiled, almost positive—from the appearance of pink rosettes on her cheeks—that Ella had meant to say a massage.

"Well, except for the bubble bath," he continued, "I would be happy with any one of those treats. But no pressure. You have a few days yet to choose my treat. *Surprise me.*"

Massimo went into the villa to shower and get dressed while Ella used the change room. As he lifted his face up to the rain shower, he thought about how comfortable he had felt, talking with Ella. *Marinella.* Joking around with her. *Having fun.*

It sent shock waves through him, igniting a shot of adrenalin throughout his veins. He *liked* being with her.

A lot.

And he had come so close to kissing her last night…

Ella had shown her vulnerability when it came to her identity, and he had been overcome with a feeling of protectiveness, wanting to enclose her within his arms and hold her tight.

With the water streaming over him, Massimo allowed the truth of the matter to sink in. The matter being feelings that he never thought he'd feel again. Happiness. *Desire. Wonder.*

She's leaving in less than a week, an inner voice reminded him. *So don't—*

Of course. He knew what the message was going to be.

Don't get any ideas. Don't start something that you know can't go anywhere. Don't put Ella in an awkward situation.

Massimo felt the momentary high he had known plummet. Like it or not, his inner voice was right. Ella would be gone in a few days. She had a personal mission to accomplish once the week was over, and then she'd be leaving Sardinia to return to Canada.

She did not seem like the kind of person who would be interested in a fling for a few days, and neither was he. Nor had he ever been while married to Rita. Whatever feelings Ella had ignited in him, he had to suppress them. Concentrate on the reason why Ella was here and get through the remainder of the week. And after his mother's birthday party and opening of the Cardiac Research Center, return to his normal routine.

Although maybe it isn't so normal…

He stepped out of the shower, toweled himself briskly and changed into jean shorts and a blue T-shirt before heading downstairs to the kitchen, determined to keep his distance from Ella, emotionally and physically…

But he had offered her a snack, so he decided to make a light frittata, since his mother would surely be orchestrating a feast for tonight's dinner. He prepared the ingredients, and when he was ready to start cooking, he glanced at the doorway, wondering what was taking Ella so long. And then he noticed a slip of paper on the granite counter.

He frowned as he read it.

I'm sorry, Massimo. I can't believe how distracted I've been. I was supposed to book a place today...

I don't want to bother you with my responsibilities, so I'm heading back to the guesthouse to take care of things. I'll have a snack there.

Thanks for the use of your pool.

Massimo reread it. Feeling deflated, he put everything he had prepared in the fridge, his appetite gone.

CHAPTER THIRTEEN

ELLA RESISTED THE urge to look back at the villa as she hurried to the guesthouse. She flopped down on the couch and stared out at the turquoise waters in the cove. But what she saw was the crystalline depths of the baron's eyes as they had joked around in the pool. The magnetic pull of them that she had found so hard to draw away from. The occasional twinkle that had caused a skip in her heartbeat.

And she hadn't been immune to his body, either.

It was obvious that Massimo worked out. It had taken every ounce of her resolve not to stare at his sculpted shoulders, arms and chest. His strong, muscled legs. The sight of him approaching the pool had given her a jolt, and later, when he had been less than a few feet away from her in the water, her nerve endings had done a frenzied dance. She had bantered with him, not wanting to reveal how his proximity was affecting her, but all the while, she had been conscious of the whitecaps swirling in her chest...

She was treading on dangerous ground.

She had never felt this way with her previous dates. Not that Massimo was a date. And not that she had taken the time, except with Dustin, to move beyond the initial couple of encounters.

Ella brushed away all thoughts of Dustin and refocused on the way she was reacting to Massimo DiLuca. And they hadn't even kissed...

Which was why the alarm signals had gone off in her brain. She had no real personal experience that she could draw upon.

How could she encourage such feelings? This was unchartered territory, and if certain situations presented themselves that put her and Massimo in close proximity, she had no idea how she would react.

Or maybe she did.

And that would be unprofessional. She was here to interview Massimo DiLuca and his mother, not to allow herself to get weak-kneed over a man.

Besides, she was leaving in a few days. Why would she want to get herself in a position where something might happen? Something she would ultimately regret?

Which was why she had decided to leave.

She would enter *Villa Serena* only to conduct the interviews from now on. And she would swim in the cove instead of the baron's pool. She'd have plenty of time to enjoy a pool at the resort she'd be booking.

Letting out a long, drawn-out sigh, Ella headed to the study, where she had left her laptop on the desk. She sat down and, moments later, scanned the list of resorts in and around Posada. After an hour of checking both resorts and B and Bs, Ella decided to stay at an *agriturismo,* a farm run by a family with a view of the Tyrrhenian Sea and private access to the beach. It was a couple of miles from Posada, but she could either rent a car or a bike if she was adventurous. The price was reasonable and she'd have a private bathroom and free Wi-Fi. Meals were optional and there was a restaurant and a pool.

The place looked absolutely charming with its pristine white stucco exterior, rounded wooden doors and balcony planters bursting with color. It was like something out of a fairy tale, its cobbled path snaking its way to the front entrance between shamrock-green manicured lawns that resembled thick, luxurious quilts.

Ella checked the booking calendar and was elated to see the following week was available. She promptly booked and paid the reservation fee and indicated that she'd take the meal plan of breakfast and a later dinner.

Sighing in relief, Ella closed her laptop. She went back to the entrance, where she had left her swim bag, and proceeded to the laundry area to wash her swimsuit. She stifled a yawn as she made herself a *panino* with fresh *mozzarella di bufala* and mushroom antipasto that she found with other jars of preserves in the pantry, which she realized was climate controlled.

The snack only made her drowsier, and realizing she was still experiencing jet lag, Ella decided to relax on the chaise lounge in the shaded section of the outdoor patio.

She closed her eyes and listened to the soothing sounds of the surf as it unfurled on the beach and then bubbled back into the sea. The scents of roses, oleander blossoms and various potted herbs wafted over to her with the gentle sea breeze, and she couldn't help feeling that she was in an enchanted garden.

The screen behind her eyelids began to display scene after scene of her trip to Sardinia, from the time she encountered the baron by almost knocking him to the ground, to the bantering between them in his pool.

He was taking too much time in her head.

She squeezed her eyes tight. And he was infiltrating her senses. Maybe she'd better go back inside and go over her notes instead of letting her imagination wander in this direction…

At the sound of a cough, she quickly sat up.

He was standing there for real, in shorts and a T-shirt. And sunglasses. He looked a little different, though…and then her gaze fell on his beard. He had trimmed it.

He nodded curtly and started to turn away but stopped to face her again.

"Did you find a place to stay?" he said huskily.

"I did. It looks lovely, the price was right, it was just the kind of unpretentious place I was looking for—" She froze, realizing how that must sound. "I didn't mean—"

"Don't worry about it," he said with a dismissive wave. "I just came by to tell you dinner will be at eight tonight at my mother's. Can you be ready by six? I'll drive the boat across, and from there, it will take another half hour by car."

"Um, sure. Oh, what should I wear? Casual or more dressy?"

Massimo's lips quirked. "Whatever you're comfortable with. Unpretentious is always good."

Massimo caught the flash of uncertainty in Ella's eyes. He probably shouldn't have said that; it made him sound like he had taken offence at her earlier comment.

"Seriously, it's not a formal event, so no ball gowns." He smiled, but she didn't reciprocate. Didn't she realize he had been teasing?

"That's good, because I left all my ball gowns at home," she said nonchalantly. "And now if you'll excuse me, I have to go over my notes from this morning."

"Of course," he said, his smile fading. She had tried to soften her tone, but she hadn't completely succeeded. *"Arrivederci."* He waved, and moments later, before passing through Oleander Lane, or *Via degli Oleandri*, as he called the path leading to his villa, he turned his head to glance back, but Ella had already disappeared into the guesthouse.

He felt a hint of disappointment...and confusion. She had seemed relaxed earlier in the pool, and comfortable joking around with him. What had happened to change her mood?

With almost two hours wait time before they had to leave, Massimo decided to go over his work email and then check the updates on the Maddalena Island resort. There were cameras set up at different spots on the exterior and interior of the building so he could virtually view the daily progress that was being made.

He was happy to see what had been accomplished since his last physical visit to the site. The project should be completed by the end of the month. He liked to choose a new architectural firm for each new resort, selecting not only the best in Italy but around the world. One of the firms that had caught his interest a few years earlier was a Canadian company that had won a prestigious award for its ecological initiatives. He had subsequently enlisted one of their teams to be in charge of the landscaping and rooftop gardens at the Maddalena resort.

What Massimo hadn't decided upon yet was the name of the resort. He had fiddled around with a few possibilities, *Mare e Meraviglia* being one of them, liking the way Sea and Wonder evoked a place of enchantment. He reached for the notepad and doodled some sketches with the two Ms intertwined, adding waves and a beach. He wondered if he should add the usual D for DiLuca in the design and then decided against it. Maybe the two Ms but with a change of the second word. *Mare e Magia*. Sea and Magic.

And then he impulsively wrote down *Marinella* and sketched waves around her name. He felt his stomach muscles tensing as he thought about how close they had been in the pool. And how natural it had seemed for her to be there...

He shook his head as if doing so would brush away his thoughts about her. With a sigh of frustration, he pushed the notepad aside, shut down his laptop, and headed to his room.

CHAPTER FOURTEEN

ELLA SURVEYED THE two dresses she had laid out on the bed, one short, one long. The short one was a sleeveless jersey dress with a ruffle around the V-neck and a flared hem that came just above her knees. It was teal blue, one of her favorite colors. The second was a yellow floral-print wrap-around maxi, also sleeveless, with drawstring waistband.

She decided on the shorter one. It was loose and comfortable, and she had a pair of teal blue sapphire earrings that matched perfectly. Hanging up the floral maxi dress, Ella felt a current of anticipation run through her, thinking about her meeting with *baronessa* Silvia DiLuca. Would she be down to earth? Arrogant? Controlling? Massimo had called her *the phenomenon that is my mother*. That sounded positive. Hopefully the evening would go well...

Why wouldn't it?

Ella was curious to see and chat with the woman, who was obviously a powerhouse, having reached such a level of success with the resort business she had started with her late husband.

Ella checked the time on her phone. She had several hours to go over her notes and recordings, work on her piece, and review the questions she had for the *baronessa* tonight, either before or after dinner. But first, she'd grab a cool drink...

Minutes later she was in the study, notes and recorder on one side of the massive desk and her laptop open and turned on. She began replaying the first recording with the intention of pausing regularly to transcribe the text, but as Massimo's voice came on, Ella found herself riveted by the sound of his voice. She leaned back in the burgundy leather office chair and just listened. At some point, she closed her eyes and as Massimo talked about his father, she picked up some inflections and nuances that she hadn't been aware of when they were actually doing the interview. When the first session came to an end, she started, feeling as if she had snapped back to consciousness after being hypnotized.

Massimo's voice had been hypnotizing...

It had lulled her with its deep timbre and

occasional huskiness, and as she had listened, she had found herself visualizing his face: his flashing eyes, the curve of his smile, his brow furrowing, his fingers stroking his jaw as he thought about his response.

Ella felt a heaviness in the air and took a long sip of her iced lemonade. There was definitely an increase in humidity from the morning.

Or was it a spike in her body temperature from listening to Massimo's voice?

Ella shook her head in annoyance at her rogue thoughts. Thoughts she had vowed to suppress.

For the next three hours, she concentrated on her task of transcribing the recording and then continued working on the piece she had started the day before. Finally, she shut down her laptop and after reviewing her questions for the *baronessa* on her notepad, she stood up and stretched, contented with what she had accomplished. She checked the time and realized she should be getting ready. She set her recorder and notepad on the credenza near the entrance. Hurrying up the spiral staircase and in the shower moments later, Ella mused over the evening ahead with the *baronessa*, immediately redirecting her thoughts when they veered in the direction of the baron…

After drying her hair and styling it in loose curls, Ella slipped on the teal blue dress and surveyed herself in the mirror. She liked the way the flared hem moved with her. Smiling, she put on the drop earrings. *Perfect*. Not too casual nor too dressy.

Her pulse spiked at the sound of a doorbell. She had thought it funny Massimo would have had one installed, given the fact that he was the only one on the island… But then again, maybe he had planned to rent it out one day or let a friend visit. At the second ring, Ella quickly put on a pair of low-heeled pumps and headed downstairs to answer the door.

When she opened it, she was slightly breathless from rushing down, and she stood blinking at the baron, too close to him to give him the once-over.

"Hello." They said it at the same time.

"You look…very nice," he said, his dark eyes focused on her face.

"Thanks. You, too." The words slipped out. She had *not* meant to say "you, too." "I mean, you look…" Good God, why was she even trying to explain? "…fine," she finished limply.

Massimo chuckled. "I'll take *fine*, although it seems like I've been downgraded from *very nice*."

Ella felt her cheeks tingle. She shifted her attention to her notepad and recorder on the credenza. "I'll just be a minute to grab my bag." She had forgotten it in the loft. And she had a second bag containing a gift for the *baronessa*, a print by the late Canadian First Nations woodland-school artist Daphne Odjig, a pioneer in developing indigenous art in Canada. Ella had traveled to Manitoulin Island, Odjig's place of birth, and had wanted to choose a gift that represented the spirit of Canada's First Peoples... In fact, the name *Manitoulin* meant *spirit island* in the Ojibwe language.

As Ella turned away, the tingling in her cheeks intensified as she imagined Massimo's gaze following her up the spiral staircase. When she returned, she saw that he hadn't budged and was watching her intently as she descended.

He held the door open for her, and minutes later, they were in Massimo's speedboat, skimming across the calm sea. Ella couldn't help glancing at Massimo's profile, his eyes narrowed in concentration and his mouth occasionally tilting upward. She wondered what he was thinking...

Maybe she shouldn't have bristled earlier when he had made the comment about wearing something unpretentious. She had assumed that he was deliberately emphasizing her gaffe, and she had taken offence. Which was ridiculous, really, since if anyone should have taken offence, it should have been *him*.

Well, it seemed that he didn't have anything he wanted to say now...

And she couldn't bring herself to make small talk. Ella bit her lip at the awkwardness between them, feeling the tension radiate throughout her body.

He suddenly turned to glance at her. *"Tutto bene?"* he said, slowing down the engine.

"Uh, yes, *sì*, everything's fine," she blurted the white lie.

"I hope you're not preoccupied about meeting my mother. She's very easy...uh..."

"Easygoing?" Ella couldn't help smiling inwardly.

"Yes, that's it. Easygoing." He chuckled. "And very hospitable...just like her son." He flashed Ella a grin. "But she's the better cook."

Ella felt her tension dissipating and her pulse quickening simultaneously. It was the way his eyes crinkled along with his perfect smile.

Moments later, when they reached the dock at *Villa Paradiso*, Massimo moored the vessel and offered Ella his hand as she stepped out of the boat. He had put his sunglasses back on.

She took his hand, liking the feel of his strong grip.

When he let go and started walking toward the parked vehicles, she followed, looking for the SUV that he had picked her up in. She spotted it, but as they approached it, Massimo paused suddenly and then strode past it, stopping at the passenger side of a silver-gray Lamborghini. Its smooth, streamlined shape, with its distinctive angles and curves, took her breath away. It reminded her of a stealth jet. *Sleek and sexy,* she couldn't help thinking. *Just like its owner...*

"*Prego,*" he said, opening the door for her, with another pulse-activating smile.

Massimo felt a surge in his chest as he let his Huracán release its potential on the Strada Statale 131, the state highway toward Cagliari. This latest vehicle purchase had been his treat to himself after moving into his villa. And it wasn't because he wanted to flaunt his wealth or be pretentious. He had simply loved the look and feel of it, unleashing its power on the long strip of highway like a predator in hot pursuit of its prey.

Letting it rip had been like giving vent to all his primal instincts, releasing the powder keg that had been building up inside him after the death of his wife. Its engine thrumming in his ears had reverberated throughout his body, just like now, making his heart race along with it.

Massimo sensed Ella's excitement, and her gasp at every acceleration made his heart pound harder. She was the first woman he had taken for a ride in his Huracán. The first woman he had *wanted* to take for a ride…

As he maneuvered through a curve, Ella's hand shot out and clasped his thigh. He had already reduced his speed, but he decreased it even further, knowing there was no vehicle imminently approaching from behind.

"Sorry," she squeaked, her voice several octaves higher. She pulled her hand away. "I thought we were going to spin out of control."

"Sorry, I didn't mean to scare you, Ella," he said, glancing quickly at her. "But let me reassure you I had complete control. We're approaching the city limits of Cagliari now, so I'll behave…and my mother's villa is another thirty-five kilometers away. We'll be there very soon."

As her eyes widened, Massimo gave her a mischievous grin. "Would *you* like to drive?"

Ella blinked at him as if he had lost all sanity. "Uh, no, thank you. I'll leave the navigation to you, since I don't have any experience in flying a jet."

He let out a deep laugh. "*Va bene.* But admit

it, the flight was exciting." He merged into the city traffic and shortly stopped at a red light.

"It *was*," she said, and for several moments, their eyes locked.

The honking of a vehicle behind them made Massimo realize the traffic light had turned green. He turned his attention reluctantly back on the road.

What was it about this woman that drew him to her?

You know... an inner voice said pointedly.

He felt his abdomen muscles tensing. Yes, he *did* know. She made him remember that he was a man...

But what was the point of acknowledging it? Whatever feelings were beginning to germinate in his consciousness, Massimo knew he couldn't allow them to grow. *How could he?* She would be leaving in four days. Whatever emotions she had been able to resuscitate in him, whether she knew it or not, he'd have to ensure that they wouldn't see the light of day.

With his reduction of speed in the town limits, Ella had relaxed, and Massimo noticed her leaning back and taking in the sweeping views with a smile. When he pulled into his mother's serpentine driveway, she straightened and reached for her seat belt.

He clicked on a remote device that he kept

in each vehicle and watched as the ornate gates to his mother's villa opened noiselessly. There were no parked vehicles except those of his mother's. Her chef had finished his part of the feast, Massimo thought, smiling. And his mother would have spent a good part of the day concocting all kinds of Sardinian delights with which to regale Ella.

The Huracán glided through, and moments later, Massimo parked it in one of the available spots next to his mother's Alfa Romeo Giulia and her Mercedes minivan. He smiled. His mother was a classy lady, with or without her fine cars and luxurious tastes. She had a kind heart and made a lot of substantial donations to charities, without fanfare. She was especially devoted to children's causes.

Massimo let his hands slide down from the wheel. "Are you ready to meet my *mamma*?"

Ella nodded and tilted her head to look out the window, but not before Massimo had caught a slight creasing of her brow. Was she thinking about *her* biological mother? He felt a twinge in his chest, imagining how difficult it had to be, knowing your mother gave you up for adoption but not knowing why.

Maybe one day Ella would return to Sardinia to try to find out.

He checked his watch. "Shall we go in?" he

said. "My mouth's already watering, thinking about the feast she has prepared." He clicked open his door to climb out and, in several strides, was at Ella's door.

She reached for her work bag and the gift bag and moments later, they were walking side by side toward the arched carved-wood door of his mother's villa.

CHAPTER FIFTEEN

ELLA HAD TO struggle to keep her jaw from dropping as she stood in the baronessa's spacious foyer with its gleaming Murano chandelier fashioned like a bouquet of cascading blue irises.

Silvia DiLuca welcomed Ella in Italian, followed by a few words in English and a warm hug. She had striking features, dark hair arranged in a braided bun and the same almond-shaped eyes as her son, with long lashes. She wore a loose peach silk blouse with olive green palazzo pants.

She wanted to take Ella on a quick tour of the house, then get the interview done in the gardens. "And then I feed you," she laughed before hugging both Ella and Massimo, who was smiling indulgently at her.

"I'll be waiting for you ladies in the living room, enjoying the soccer game," Massimo said wryly. *"Divertitevi."*

"Of course we will have fun," his mother retorted, slapping him none too gently on his backside as he strode away.

He turned and gave a deep laugh. "You're lucky you're my mother," he teased, and then gave Ella a wink.

Ella followed the *baronessa* through the main floor of the sprawling villa, her cheeks tingling. The way Massimo had looked at her had caused her heart to flutter. No, not flutter, *flip*.

Her brain and heart were clashing, and for a few moments she was listening to their arguments. Her common sense was telling her that she was foolishly falling for the baron. Her heart was urging her to feel whatever she was feeling, to be open to...

Don't even go there, her brain ordered. *You're leaving. There's no possibility of that happening. Besides, it's a one-way feeling, girl. He's not ready for lo—*

"Ella, this is my kitchen."

The *baronessa* entered the massive room, complete with a real wood-burning hearth and an island that was longer than Ella's apartment kitchen. "What a beautiful room!" Ella smiled. "And whatever you're cooking smells wonderful!"

"Please, you call me Silvia, *va bene*? Now I take you to my gardens."

Outside, Ella drew in her breath. "This is an absolute Garden of Eden," she said. "How enchanting."

Silvia led her through themed gardens that were meticulously designed and partitioned by boxwood hedges and featured marble statues and fountains, citrus trees and pergolas, and flower varieties Ella had never seen before. One area was exclusively for herbs and resembled a monastic garden with its terra-cotta planters and cobblestone paths. Everywhere she looked, Ella spotted a different variety of tree: palm, prickly pear, cypress, lemon, mandarin and persimmon.

They stopped at a serene park-like section with a pond shaded by giant palm trees, and Silvia motioned for Ella to sit opposite her on one of the ornate benches.

Ella took her recorder out of her bag, and after opening her notepad to the interview questions, clicked it on. She smiled at the *baronessa*, feeling relaxed, not only because of the peaceful ambiance of the gardens but because of the twinkle in those dark brown eyes, eyes that her son had inherited.

The hour flew by, and Ella was pleased with the responses Silvia had given her, clearly demonstrating not only her business savvy but her community-minded initiatives and her charitable acts. Her voice had wavered when she conveyed how important the DiLuca Cardiac Research Center was to her and Massimo, and Ella had felt her heart twinge, thinking of how mother and son were channeling their grief in ways that would ultimately help so many others. And then the *baronessa* had winked at Ella and enthusiastically brought up her upcoming birthday party.

Ella put away her recorder and notepad in her bag, and they started walking back to the villa.

"Who or what inspired you to create these lovely gardens?" She smiled across at Massimo's mother.

"It was my husband," Silvia said softly. Speaking in both Italian and halting English, she told Ella how he had supported her love of art and design and had encouraged her to plan the gardens at their first resort. She had ended up designing all of them. "He was a wonderful man who understood my passion," she said wistfully, her gaze shifting to her grounds. Suddenly she turned to Ella. "What is *your* passion, Ella? Do *you* have a wonderful man in your life?"

Massimo strode to the huge window overlooking the gardens. He had spotted Ella and his mother earlier sitting by the pond and had smiled at his mother's animated hand movements. She was no doubt talking about her two passions, her gardens and cooking. He couldn't see their faces clearly or hear their conversation, but Ella was leaning forward, and through the open shutters, he heard their occasional shared laughter.

Forty minutes later, Roberta, his mother's dining server, set out the appetizers, a variety of local cheeses and spiced olives, and a special Sardinian bread called *carta da musica*— thin, crispy rounds resembling sheets of music parchment. Afterward, they enjoyed the *culurgiones* his mother had made, ravioli with a filling of sweet potato and pecorino served with a butter-sage sauce. The main course was fennel-encrusted swordfish with asparagus spears drizzled with olive oil and sea salt.

After the dessert of *amarettus*—the Sardinian word for *amaretti* made with bitter almonds and lemon peel—and *sebadas*, Ella leaned back with a contented sigh, which made his mother chuckle. "Now you know why the interview came first, Ella."

They left shortly after coffee and liqueurs and the usual hugs from his mother. She and Ella had embraced, as well, with his mother murmuring *"Buona notte, cara"* to her.

The evening air was hot and humid, and when they were in his car, Massimo turned on the air conditioner. "I have a feeling we might get some rain tonight," he said. "Hopefully we'll be back home before then."

"Mmm…" she replied.

He glanced at Ella as he fastened his seat belt. She seemed much more relaxed than before. Mellow, actually. It could have been the shot of *mirto* she had tried, an amber Sardinian liqueur made from myrtle berries. He had declined it in favor of a second espresso, but he felt rather mellow himself. A combination of the great food. *And company.*

"I gather your interview with my mother went well."

Ella turned to him. "Very well," she said with a smile. "Your mother was a pleasure to interview." She chuckled. "Not at all a dragon."

He let out a deep laugh. "You must have made a positive impression on her. Correction… I know you made a great impression on her."

She looked at him curiously. "How do you know?"

He didn't answer right away as he made his way through the villa gates. Once they closed behind him, he said, "*Mamma* has always claimed to have a certain intuition about people. She sensed it with you right away."

Ella's brow creased. "How would you know that?"

"She only takes her best friends or people she feels she can trust into her gardens. That is her sacred space. Her private space. Ordinarily she would conduct an interview in her study." He came to a stop sign. "Trust me," he said, flashing her a smile before driving on. "I know my mother."

"Well… I'm flattered," Ella murmured.

"I'm not trying to flatter you, Ella."

She didn't reply, and his quick glance in her direction caught her puzzled—or maybe hurt—expression as she turned to look out her window.

"That didn't come out right," he said, wishing he could just park the car and talk to her face-to-face. But he couldn't risk wasting time if he wanted to get back to the villa before the downpour.

"What I meant to say was I'm not telling you this to boost your ego, Ella. I'm telling you this because it's the truth." Out of the corner of his eye, he saw her turn to look at him. "And one more thing…she said, *'Buona notte, cara,'* to you. She doesn't use that term lightly. There's only one other person she called a *dear*."

"Your father?"

"No. She called him *amore*." He swallowed. "She called my late wife Rita, *cara*."

Massimo felt a surprising relief once he told Ella this, as if a buildup of pressure inside him had been released.

His mother liked Ella.

And so did he. He didn't see it as a betrayal to Rita for either one of them. Rita would always have a place in his mother's heart. And his.

But had his admission made Ella uncomfortable? Is that why she hadn't said anything? He ventured a quick glance at her.

She was smiling at him.

Feeling a surge inside his chest, he grinned back and merged onto the freeway, anxious to get back to *Villa Serena*. Ella gasped as the Huracán accelerated and her hand shot out and landed on his leg.

And it seemed to rest there for a while before she pulled it away...

When they arrived at the Paradiso, Massimo looked at the gathering clouds. "We should be able to make it back before the rain starts," he told her. They would be fine in the boat's cabin, but he didn't like the idea of driving the boat at night in a heavy rain.

A quarter of a mile away from his villa, they heard the first rumblings of thunder. Ella turned to him, her eyes wide. He increased his speed, and the rain began pelting the boat just as he was docking. He held out a hand to Ella and she clambered out. "How fast can you run?" he said.

"Faster than you can swim," she teased.

He clasped her hand tightly as they dashed toward the villa, but halfway there, the rain turned into a downpour with the boom of thunder reverberating around them. They reached the villa entrance just as jagged spears of lightning branded the sky.

Inside the lit foyer, they stood dripping, and as they caught the reflection of their faces in the oval mirror, they both started to laugh. "I'll go grab some towels in a minute," he said, unbuttoning his shirt. After taking it off, he squeezed the excess water out and used it to wipe his face and head. He noticed that Ella was trying not to stare, but their gazes met several times.

She couldn't very well take her dress off, and because of the height of the mirror, she probably hadn't been aware of the fact her loose-fitting garment was now clinging to her provocatively, highlighting the curves and shadows that had been previously concealed.

The soft but quick beat of his heart seemed to suddenly match the boom of thunder that made Ella jump, seconds before the lights went out. His arms instinctively shot up to steady her. In the darkness, feeling her wet, shivering body against him, his arms wrapped around her as if they had a will of their own. Her breath fanned his Adam's apple, igniting a sizzle through him that coincided with the series of lightning flashes that illuminated them briefly through the villa windows.

Ella didn't move. Massimo closed his eyes, his chest heaving, allowing himself to just experience the moment. *The feeling.* The wonder of his whole being, body and soul, wanting to…to…

Her lips brushed against his jaw. With a groan that was muffled by the next clap of thunder, his hand slid up to cup the back of her head while his lips found hers. He froze for a moment as they made contact, and then he lingered, first over her lower and then her top lip. Ella's hands reached upward to trace a path on his back, and the way her fingers moved over him, giving a slight squeeze every few seconds, was threatening to undo him.

At her sudden intake of breath, he pressed her tightly against him and kissed her deeply, his heart clanging wildly when she reciprocated.

Massimo could taste the myrtle liqueur on her tongue. His pulse skyrocketed. His hands dropped to blindly find the hem of her dress, without breaking off the kiss. His fingers trembled as they closed over the drenched material…

And then the lights flickered back on.

It was like getting a bucket of cold water poured over his head. He released the hold on her dress, and as the kiss ended, they stood looking at each other, both dazed.

He didn't know whether he should apologize or kiss her again.

"Ella—"

"I—I have to go," she said, crossing her arms self-consciously in front of her.

They could both hear the rain pelting the villa's tiled roof and windows, followed by a menacing series of thunderclaps.

"You can't leave now, with this storm," he said huskily. "The path down to the guesthouse will be too dangerous. And there are too many trees that are a target for lightning." His eyes narrowed. "You'll have to spend the night."

CHAPTER SIXTEEN

ELLA WATCHED HIM disappear around the corner after telling her that he would return with some towels.

She loved storms…as long as she was inside. She'd watch a deluge from the window seat in her bedroom and wait for the lightning to sizzle across the night sky.

This storm would have been amazing to watch from the guesthouse, with the stupendous views of the cove, but she wasn't about to head there after Massimo's warning.

He was right. It *was* too dangerous to go out. But what was even more dangerous was the storm inside her. And she couldn't put the blame entirely on the baron. Or the weather, although running up to the villa with her hand in his had certainly started it. Followed by Massimo taking off his shirt, the ear-splitting boom of thunder that had caused her to practically jump in his arms and the lights switching off.

Pressed up against him in the dark and feeling the touch of Massimo's hands and lips had ignited a yearning within her that she hadn't been able to suppress. His kiss had been powerful... *seismic*. If it hadn't actually caused the floor to split and quake around her, it certainly had shaken her to the core.

But the return of the electricity had shocked her back to reality...to the knowledge that allowing anything further to develop would be a big mistake. Just allowing herself to be kissed by the baron—*and kissing him back*—had not been the wisest thing to do. It had never happened in the past with a client, and she could not let it happen again.

No matter how physically attracted she was to him.

No matter that being in his sphere made her pulse spike in a way she had never experienced with Dustin or the other guys she had dated.

And despite her earlier feeling that Massimo wouldn't be interested in her, his lips and his body were telling her something different.

It didn't matter.

She had to choose reason over recklessness.

Simply because she would be leaving soon, and the last thing she wanted was to complicate matters by giving in to what her body seemed to be yearning for.

Ella shivered. If only they had arrived ten minutes earlier… She would be in the guesthouse, comfortably watching the storm in her robe, instead of standing here soaking wet in a dress that had become too revealing for comfort.

And now she had no choice but to spend the night under his roof.

The lights flickered as the baron returned with several extra-large towels. He had changed into a black T-shirt and jeans. He handed two towels to Ella and dropped one on the floor where he had been standing. She wrapped one around her body and used the other one for her hair.

"I'll take you to a guest room," he said brusquely, as if he were a resort employee speaking to a paying guest. "It has an en suite bathroom, if you'd like to take a warm shower. And there's a bathrobe on the hook behind the sliding door. There are hangers for your wet clothes in the walk-in closet." He handed her a bag. "Slippers, since your shoes are soaked."

Ella followed him past his living room and up the grand staircase to the second level.

"Buona notte," he said, giving her a curt nod. "I've put a bottle of water on the night table. If you need anything else, just let me know. My room is at the end of the hall."

"Thank you," she murmured stiffly, avoiding his gaze as she entered the room. "Good night."

She clicked the door shut without looking back. Realizing that she was still shivering, she hurried to the washroom and ,moments later, felt the soothing jets of warm water ease some of the tension from her body.

Much as Ella wanted to linger, she made it a quick shower instead and, minutes later, after drying her hair, climbed into the king-size bed. The shutters were open and she could see and hear the downpour, feeling her usual excitement at the continual rumblings of thunder and the intermittent flashes of lightning.

The deluge had brought with it a refreshing breeze, and Ella shivered, still feeling the electricity of Massimo's kiss.

She would have to forget that kiss while conducting the remaining interviews.

And during the *baronessa*'s birthday and the grand opening of the DiLuca Cardiac Research Center.

The pelting rain had changed to a soft and steady flow, and her glance shifted to the balcony. Maybe she'd be able to sleep if she closed the shutters. Maybe the darkness would help erase the image of Massimo from her mind.

As Ella strode to the balcony, lightning streaked the sky, followed by a deafening thunderclap. She let out a shriek. And then the rain intensified and she quickly closed the balcony doors and the shutters.

A shaft of light appeared, and Ella turned to her partially open door.

"Ella, are you okay?" Massimo wasn't visible, but she could hear the genuine alarm in his voice.

"I'm fine. It was the thunder—it scared me half to death." Ella grabbed her robe and put it on. "I think it's going to take me a while before I can—"

Another rumble drowned out her words.

"How about a cup of tea? *Una camomilla?* I guarantee that will make you fall asleep."

"Um, well… Okay, thank you."

He hadn't been able to sleep, either. But it hadn't been the rain or the thunder. It was the memory of Ella in his arms, his lips on hers…

As they walked downstairs, Massimo couldn't help thinking how natural it felt, the two of them heading to the kitchen in their bathrobes to make a pot of soothing chamomile tea.

"Make yourself comfortable in the living area," he told her. When he set down a tray on the coffee table a couple of minutes later, he found Ella sitting on the sectional looking through one of his books on the festivals of Sardinia. She looked up at him. "I know so little of my country of birth," she murmured. "The history, the traditions, the dialect…"

"That will start to change in a few days once you meet your uncle," Massimo said, pouring her chamomile tea.

"I'm not sure if I should disrupt his or his family's lives with a sudden appearance," she said, stirring in some honey.

"But you are his family. Don't you think your uncle would want to see you, know that you're well after all these years?" he said, hearing the urgency in his voice.

Ella looked across at Massimo, her brow wrinkling. "I…imagine he would. But if I connect with him, it might lead to…other things."

Massimo knew he was nudging her into a sensitive area of her life, but he told himself he was doing it to help her.

"Like finding out about your biological mother and father?" Massimo said quietly.

"My mother, actually." She traced the rim of her cup with her finger. "She never revealed who the father—my father—was. The papers listed him as *straniero*."

"A foreigner." Massimo said curtly.

Ella set her cup down with a trembling hand. "In any case, I can't see that happening. If there was any way of finding out more about her, wouldn't my adoptive mother have told me?"

"She might not have wanted to explore that, especially after moving back to Canada after the trauma of losing her husband," Massimo said gently. "And maybe she was waiting for *you* to indicate your desire to find your birth mother. In any case, there are ways now…"

"That would be opening a Pandora's box," Ella said, shaking her head adamantly. "I don't think I'm ready to deal with that now, especially since I'll only be here for a week after this assignment." She bit her lip. "I just want to enjoy a week of sun and sand before heading back home. And if during my week, I decide to try to contact my uncle, then I will."

"Are you happy with your life back home?" he murmured.

Where was he going with this?

"As happy as I can be," she said curtly, not bothering to curb the defensiveness in her voice. "I've got a great job. I get to travel and enjoy perks most people would love to have." Her brows arched. "Are you happy with *your* life? I mean—"

Massimo's eyes narrowed. "To quote someone I know, 'As happy as I can be,' given the circumstances."

"I get the impression that you could be happier," she ventured.

"I get the same impression. About *you*," he said.

He saw Ella take a deep breath. "You can tell me to mind my own business, but...but maybe you might be ready to...to be with people again."

Did she really mean a woman?

A knot settled in his throat and he couldn't reply immediately. The reality of his life hit him. Hard.

He was alone.

He had everything he could possibly want that his money could buy.

But he didn't have a woman who would love him for himself, not his billions. And he didn't have a child...or children.

He glanced at Ella. Something in the depths of her eyes was inviting him to keep talking.

"Three years ago, I vowed to stay single, unable to bear the thought of...of being with another woman," he began haltingly. "I was certain that I would never be able to love again. All the emotions I had experienced with Rita vanished from my life along with her, leaving a dark, empty space." He paused, remembering how he had felt the vacuum in his chest every day, the only visitors being grief, shock and disbelief that happiness and love had been snatched away from him.

"I wanted to hide from the world, cringing at things I had enjoyed with Rita, like strolling by market stalls in a piazza, walking along a beach at night. Or holiday shopping." The sound of Christmas music months after she passed had sent pain spiraling through him. "I couldn't take the laughter of groups enjoying lunch on a restaurant patio. Their carefree chatter just emphasized what was lacking in my own life. So I did everything possible to stay away from people."

He told Ella how he had become increasingly reclusive and had grown a beard. And when he did go out, he'd deliberately dress in casual clothes with a cap and glasses to further disguise himself.

"I just wanted to hide from the world. Mourn my lost dreams." He felt the backs of his eyes prickling. "I realize now, Ella, that if I want to be happy again, I have to make new dreams. With new people."

Massimo swallowed the jagged lump in his throat. He set down his cup and leaned forward, his hands under his chin. "I know we haven't had exactly the same experience, Ella, but we've both suffered loss in our lives. *Great loss.* You took a big step in coming to Sardinia, and now you have a chance to gain something. *Someone.*"

He stood up and went around the coffee table to sit next to her.

"Now *you* can tell me to mind *my* own business…but I think it would be good to call your uncle while you're here. Make that connection. After tomorrow's interview, I'll be happy to drive you to where you'll be staying and take you around the area so you're familiar with the town."

He grasped her hand and gazed earnestly into her eyes. "And if you'd like, Marinella, I'll come with you to find your uncle and his family, if he has one. *Va bene?*" He squeezed her hand lightly. "I think you need to find *your* people, and you're right about *me* needing to be with people again, too."

CHAPTER SEVENTEEN

ELLA HAD FELT her heart begin to thump erratically when Massimo had sat next to her. Now she was trying to process her jumbled thoughts about what he had just told her. Was he inferring about being open to letting others into his life? Like her?

She blinked at him wordlessly for a few seconds. He was offering to accompany her in her personal business. That was something friends did.

Was he offering to be a friend? And after sharing that scorching kiss, *could* they be just friends?

Her gaze dropped to her hand that he still held. And then she looked up at him again to search the depths of his eyes for answers. He must have sensed her hesitation, for he gently withdrew his hand. "I don't want to stick my nose in your business…if you don't want me to, Ella."

"You...you must have more important matters to take care of with your own business," she replied hesitantly.

"I can take a day off from my business," he said with a smirk. "Anytime I choose. And the boss—you've heard of that elusive fellow, *barone* Massimo DiLuca—he's pretty reasonable, when I have a good excuse."

Ella felt the corners of her mouth lifting. "What about the *baronessa*?" she said. "She might have something to say about her son shirking his duties..."

Massimo let out a deep laugh. "*Baronessa* Silvia *is* a dragon when it comes to business matters," he said, his eyes crinkling. "Or she wouldn't have got to where she is with DiLuca Resorts. But I happen to have heard that she has quite a soft spot for her wonderful—and extremely handsome—son."

Ella burst out laughing. "Maybe her wonderful son has a face only a mother would love."

As they laughed together, Ella felt warmth radiating throughout her nerve endings. And in Massimo's eyes.

This was exactly what friends did. Laugh and joke around. But there was something more. She couldn't pull her eyes away from him...and he was looking at her with a tenderness she had never seen in the eyes of any of her dates in the past. He didn't have to say anything. He was showing her that he cared.

Something leaped in her heart. She was home. In Sardinia. And soon, she could be— *would be*—connecting with a member or members of her own family. Massimo was right.

She suddenly realized how much she really wanted to do this...*had* to do this.

And she hoped her *zio* Domenicu and any or all other members would welcome her and accept her in their lives. Because if she was sure of one thing, now that she'd had a taste of her homeland, it was that she was ready to return. She had a history here, even though she still had to discover much of it. This was her *motherland*.

Suddenly Massimo put his arm around her, and she let her head rest against his chest. "We'd better get some sleep," he murmured, his breath fanning her cheek. "I think it would be better to head out early to Posada. We can have the interview on the drive there, otherwise there won't be enough time to do everything I want to do...with you."

Massimo embraced Ella at her bedroom door. He didn't want to meet her gaze. And weaken...

"Buona notte, Marinella," he said, and turned away, forcing himself to keep on walking until he was in his own room. He shut the door and strode to his balcony. The rain had subsided along with the humidity, leaving a light breeze in its place. The sea had calmed, and he listened to the gentle gush of the tide's ebb and flow. Gentle yet sensuous in the dark...

Massimo breathed in deeply, trying to process the emotions swirling in his head. He hadn't seen this coming. He hadn't expected to have the deepest recesses of his heart revived. By a foreigner who wasn't a foreigner. A woman who shared the same heritage.

Yet up to now, he hadn't felt the desire—or need—to be open to a friendship—*let alone relationship*—with another woman, Sardinian or otherwise. What was it about this Marinella Rossi that had managed to find an opening in the protective barricade around his heart?

Massimo glanced up at the sky. The clouds had mostly dispersed, allowing the stars to pierce through the blackness. He thought about Rita, and the star directly above him seemed to glow brighter. Something many of the older generations of southern Italians, Sardinians and Sicilians included, would believe a sign from heaven. He didn't consider himself to be superstitious in that way, but as he watched the star for a few moments, he sensed Rita would be happy for him.

"*Grazie,*" he murmured and went inside. He set his phone alarm and tossed his robe on the ottoman at the foot of his bed before getting under the covers. Closing his eyes, he listened to the rush of the tide, savoring the peace in his heart.

CHAPTER EIGHTEEN

ELLA HADN'T BEEN able to sleep right away. She'd worked on her developing story for the magazine, inserting some of the points she had jotted into her notepad. And then she had surveyed the series of questions for the next interview, which would be conducted in Massimo's Lamborghini instead of his villa.

Finally, she had put her work aside and had gone to bed with a bubbly feeling. *Like champagne,* she had thought with a wry smile, *ready to spill over with excitement.* Massimo had reached out to her, offering to accompany her to a meeting with her uncle, and she had been relieved she wouldn't have to go alone. Although she didn't think that she had actually told him yes.

In bed, Ella had thought about connecting with her uncle once she finished her assignment for the magazine. She had *zio* Domenicu's number and address—and once she discovered if he would be open to having her visit, she'd make arrangements to go there. But since Massimo had offered to take her to Posada, she had decided she might as well summon up her courage and call her uncle the next morning.

Now, waking up to bands of sunlight streaming through the open shutters of her balcony, Ella felt a flutter of mingled excitement and anxiety. She checked the time and decided she'd attempt a call to her uncle before going down for breakfast. She dressed quickly, all while going over what she'd say in her head. She reached for her cell phone, and finding Zio Domenicu's number in the contacts, she called it with trembling fingers.

After a few rings, she was ready to hang up, losing her nerve. And then someone picked up. *"Pronto."*

The voice was younger than what she had expected to hear. So maybe her *zio* had married and had children. This "child" sounded like a young man. He would be her cousin. She swallowed hard. *"Buongiorno. C'è il signor Rossi? Domenicu Rossi?"*

There was a pause on the other line. Ella's heart thudded, filling her eardrums.

"Chi parla?" The voice had become a little sharper.

"Mi chiamo Ella," she said, the backs of her

eyes beginning to sting. *"Marinella... Rossi. Siamo parenti..."*

Telling her cousin that she was a relative resulted in a longer pause. And then he called out excitedly to his father. *"Papà! Papà! Vieni subito!"*

And moments later, she was talking, her *zio* was crying, and after she told him that she would be in Posada for a week, there were more tears. By this time, he had her on speakerphone and the rest of the family—big or small—was chattering excitedly among themselves, especially when she said that she'd be visiting the area to check out the place she had booked.

Her uncle immediately insisted she stay with *them*. Ella didn't want to hurt his feelings, but she told him she didn't want to impose and that they could talk more later in the afternoon after her friend drove her to the farmhouse. She didn't have the heart to tell him that returning to the place she had spent the first four years of her life might be too much for her and she would have to take it step by step...

Ella blew out her breath slowly after she said goodbye and turned off her phone. She hadn't expected to be doing this before the *baronessa*'s birthday. But now that she had made the connection, her spirits were soaring.

Her uncle had sounded thrilled at her call, as had the rest of his family. *Her family.*

Feeling as if she had won a lottery jackpot, Ella skipped lightly down the stairs, her nostrils taking in the smell of coffee. There was something about the way an Italian espresso filled a room with such an aromatic scent.

She couldn't wait to tell Massimo.

He turned when she entered the kitchen, his gaze sweeping over her. She halted in her tracks. He had shaved off his beard, leaving just a light scruff on his upper lip and face. If he had been handsome before, now he looked...*gorgeous.*

She couldn't help giving him a once-over, as well. Tan, belted Bermuda shorts and a tailored white short-sleeved shirt that he wore tucked in. Fitted and fabulous...

"Buongiorno, Marinella."

Her head snapped back up. *"Buongiorno*, Massimo."

"Cappuccino?"

"Sì, grazie." She took a place at the kitchen island, and when he set down her cappuccino, she thanked him again and told him about contacting her cousin and telling him she'd be visiting this afternoon.

He finished his espresso. "I'm happy for you," he said huskily. "I'm glad that you will be reuniting with your uncle and his—*your*—family."

Ella smiled. "I feel good about this," she admitted. "Now I have a reason to return to Sardinia…"

Massimo's smile froze. She didn't notice; she was enjoying her almond brioche. Her words revealed so much to him, mainly that Ella was focused on her family in Sardinia. Not him.

There was no reason for him to feel slighted. Or disappointed. Yet he couldn't help it. He thought they had shared something special last night. Not just an intoxicating kiss but moments of shared feelings and vulnerability.

He had obviously misunderstood. Not the kiss; he had sensed Ella's desire as much as his own, and that was normal and natural. She was a beauty, and his body hadn't been immune to that. Especially with her being in such close proximity. The lightning hadn't struck *him* during the storm, but *she* had.

And he had succumbed to more than just her physical beauty. Her intelligence, her sensitivity, and her honesty had reeled him in, as well.

But he was delusional to think—or expect—that anything could progress. After tomorrow, she would be gone. She'd still be in Sardinia, but she'd be reestablishing a connection with her *zio* Domenicu and his family, which was clearly what they both wanted.

And what do you want? an inner voice pressed.

Massimo poured himself another espresso. There was no point going there... No point at all.

It was probably a mistake to have offered to take Ella to Posada, but he couldn't very well retract his proposal now. He'd have to just get through the day and his mother's birthday tomorrow, and then they'd say their goodbyes.

"Do you have everything you need?" he said brusquely as she finished her brioche. "Or do you have to stop at the guesthouse?"

"I'd like to change before we head out, if that's okay."

He nodded. *"Non c'è problema.* I'll meet you at the dock." He stood up. "You can just text me your uncle's address."

Fifteen minutes later, Ella had changed into a pair of tangerine Capri pants and a white tank top under a floral cotton shirt. She had her hat and sunglasses on, and as she approached the speedboat, Massimo felt a tightening in his chest.

Ella held on to her sun hat as he sped away from the coast. He focused on steering, and although he sensed Ella's gaze on him several times, he deliberately avoided looking her way.

When they were in his Lamborghini and cruising on the freeway, Ella pulled out her recorder and notepad. "I doubt we'll get a good sound." She frowned. "But I'll still record you while I take notes."

"Prego." He nodded. "I'm ready when you are."

"What is it like, working with the *baronessa*?" she said. "Tell me about your work relationship…and has your mother mentioned retirement plans at all?"

Massimo flashed her a wry smile. "I'm a very lucky person, being able to work with her. She's smart, creative and generous with our employees. She listens to my ideas and vice versa. Although she's cut back on her work hours, she hasn't brought up retirement."

For the next few minutes, Massimo answered questions about his mother's birthday, after which Ella informed him she had made up a list of shots that she would like his photographer to take for the magazine. "And as you requested," she added, "you can approve them and then have them emailed to me."

She then proceeded to ask about the genesis of the Cardiac Research Center that would bear the DiLuca name.

It was a project extremely important to him and his mother, he told her. It was a long-term personal and financial commitment that would honor the memory of their loved ones, and help countless people in the future.

When they were done, Ella put away her recorder and notepad and concentrated on enjoying the scenery. She looked intently out at the stretches of farmland, exclaiming at the sight of the Rio Posada, and near the left bank of the river, in the middle of a plain, Massimo pointed out a conical prehistoric monument built with large blocks of stone.

"We're in Torpè, and this is called Nuraghe San Pietro," he said, "named after the ancient Nuraghic tribe in the region. We could stop and have a look on the way back, as I'm sure you're anxious to get to Posada."

"I'd like that," she said. "I had read about the Nuraghe and also Mount Tepilora and Tepilora Park. It looks absolutely stunning."

"Ah, yes, the home of the golden eagle and excellent hiking trails."

"I'd love to check out the trails, too...but not today," she added quickly. "My priority is to reconnect with my family."

"Of course. And that will happen very soon." He gestured at the sign ahead.

A few minutes later as they approached

Posada, Massimo pointed out the medieval village clinging to the side of a limestone cliff—its cluster of colorful homes cascading down the hillside toward the sea, like a flowing peasant skirt—and a thirteenth-century tower and ruins of the *Castello della Fava*.

"It's so beautiful," Ella said wistfully. "It looks like something out of a fairy tale."

"Which is why it has been named one of the most beautiful villages in Italy. Do you remember any of it?"

She shook her head. "I was only four when we moved to Canada. I don't have any specific memories, other than a blue door and—" her mouth curved into a smile briefly "—some chickens."

"What about people? Your relatives? Do you remember them?"

"Vaguely. But my memories might actually be getting confused with the photos my mother—Cassandra—showed me of the four years we spent in Posada."

Massimo heard the tremor in her voice. His hand reached out to clasp hers, but he withdrew it when she abruptly turned her head to look out her side window.

He felt a twist in his chest. She may not have seen his attempted gesture of empathy, but perhaps it was just as well. It was a reminder for him to stay neutral...

He began the ascent toward Posada's historic center, distracted by the groups of teenagers and people—both men and woman—who stopped and stared at his Huracán or whistled their approval. Having visited Posada before, Massimo knew where he could park privately, near a hidden scenic outlook on the mountain that he and Ella could walk to. It was worth stopping at, with its panoramic view of the countryside and endless Tyrrhenian Sea.

As they made their way up steep steps and through cobbled side streets lined by homes of ancient stone and charming stucco houses painted coral, cream, yellow or white, most having arched doorways and large glazed planters overflowing with blooms or featuring a flowering tree, Massimo felt conflicting emotions.

He was happy to be with Ella, showing her the land of her birth, but simultaneously unhappy, knowing that he had a very limited time in which to do it. There was simply too much to discover and enjoy in a day. In less than a day.

Ella gasped, as he had imagined she would when they arrived at the scenic outlook. Surprisingly, they were the only ones there.

Checking the time, he realized it was after noon and tourists were probably flocking to the restaurants all vying for their patronage.

"This. Is. Magnificent." She looked downward and Massimo heard her draw in her breath again. "Oh, look, Massimo," she said, clasping his forearm, "the beach, with the ancient watchtower and the Church of San Giovanni. I can't get over this view. The beach sand looks like a strip of caramel—and, oh, my gosh, that turquoise water... I wish I had brought my bathing suit." She squeezed his arm. "Thank you for bringing me here." And before he could respond, she impulsively gave him a hug.

CHAPTER NINETEEN

Ella realized that Massimo wasn't reciprocating the hug. She let her arms drop stiffly and stepped away from him, feeling as awkward as a teenager at her first dance. She didn't intend to ask him why he had turned into one of the stone statues they had seen in a piazza on their way to the terrace lookout. It was obvious. Now that she was officially finished interviewing him and would be leaving the day after tomorrow, he was assuming his baron demeanor, just as he had when he'd been at the airport to pick her up.

And what exactly had she expected? That he would pull her tightly to him and kiss her the way he had before?

The altitude was to blame. She felt on top of the world standing on this terrace on Mount Tepilora, and she had been temporarily swept away with a rush of pleasure at seeing an eagle's-eye view of her village, the surrounding countryside and the enchanting blue waters of the Tyrrhenian, catching the sun with every wave and mirroring the cerulean blue of the sky. This was as close to heaven as she could possibly be. And she had been filled with gratitude that Massimo had thought to bring her here. So she had hugged him. Without thinking.

But Massimo's literally cold shoulder had brought her back to earth. *Hard.* She might as well have been hugging the trunk of one of the holm oaks on the hillside. She and Massimo were realms apart. And it was obvious that he thought so, too.

The best thing to do would be to get her business done here, and then return to his island, get a good night's sleep and brace herself for her final days with the DiLucas.

She suddenly felt exhausted. And hot.

"I think we should go to my uncle's farm now," she said, keeping her voice steady, "and then we can head back to *Villa Serena.*"

She saw his brow furrow.

"You don't want to stroll around the village? What about checking out your *agriturismo*? I thought you wanted to see where you'd be staying for a week."

Ella shook her head. "It's not necessary. I'll call to let my uncle know we're on our way." She tossed her hair back and started to walk away. There would be plenty of time to stroll around during her holiday.

She couldn't let the baron ruin her day, she told herself. She had family to visit. Family who would hopefully show her warmth. And maybe even love...

Massimo had programmed the address of the farmhouse on his GPS and as they descended the hillside toward the farmland on the lower slopes, he wondered at Ella's sudden change of plans. And mood. He figured it was nerves, finally about to meet the family she was connected to by blood. He could understand wanting to make that her priority instead of sightseeing...

Her hug had caught him off guard. Before he could reciprocate—and he had wanted to, despite his intentions to stay neutral—she had backed away. Now she was staring out the side window, and he was reluctant to make conversation. She was probably going over what she wanted to say to her *zio* Domenicu. It would no doubt be a very emotional reunion.

Massimo turned into a rougher country lane and Ella suddenly swiveled around to look at the screen. "We're almost there," she murmured, and leaned forward, her eyes narrowing.

He drove slowly, passing enclosed fields of

pasture where a herd of sheep and goats were grazing at the wild grasses around the gnarled trunks of olive trees, their silver-green foliage rustling in the warm breeze. Farther along were fenced-in rows and rows of crops, interspersed with fruit and fig trees, and a series of separate sheds with enclosed pens. They saw rabbits, a sow with its litter, and a cow. And as Massimo rounded a curve, they came to the last shed—a henhouse with a clutch of chicks squabbling over seed—and a view of the country house beyond. With a blue door.

A dog started barking from an enclosure, and the blue door opened. The man standing on the doorstep started waving to them, and as Massimo came to a stop, the man began striding toward the car, a welcoming smile on his weathered face. Ella glanced at Massimo for a moment, her eyes blinking as they filled with tears, and then she opened the side door and ran out to her uncle.

CHAPTER TWENTY

"Stavo aspettando per questo momento," zio Domenicu told her, wiping his own eyes.

"Anch'io," she replied. She had been waiting for this moment, too.

"Are you going to leave your friend sitting in the car?"

"Zio! You speak English?"

"Yes, *bella.* I wanted to be prepared for my little Canadian niece when she came back." He gave her another hug. "Your family is waiting inside. But first, introduce me to your *giovanotto.*"

"He's not my young man," she wanted to reply, but her uncle was already walking toward Massimo, who had climbed out of the Huracán and was extending his hand. *"Barone* DiLuca, this is my *zio* Domenicu," she said.

"Piacere." He smiled at her uncle. "But please call me Massimo. And now that I've delivered your niece safely, I'll be on my way."

He turned to Ella. "Just text me when you're ready."

"No, no!" Domenicu said. "You are a friend of Marinella and very welcome in our home." He put up his hand. "No arguments, *giovanotto*."

Massimo laughed. "*Grazie, signor* Domenicu, but I think Marinella might want some time alone with you and your family."

Her uncle looked pointedly at her. It was obvious that he expected her to invite Massimo in. "You're welcome to stay," she said, her cheeks flushed as she met Massimo's gaze, unwilling to breach what she knew was typical Sardinian courtesy.

"Brava," her uncle said, and he put one arm over Ella's shoulder and the other over Massimo's. "Let's go inside."

As they began walking toward the entrance, the blue door burst open again and a group ran out to meet them.

"Meet your *famiglia*," Domenicu laughed, squeezing Ella's shoulder.

In the next few minutes Ella met *zio* Domenicu's wife, Lina, their daughter Maria and son-in-law, Tomasso, and Maria and Tomasso's four-year-old little girl, Angelica. They greeted Massimo with the same enthusiasm, and Ella wondered if they, too, thought that she and Massimo were a couple…

They were ushered inside where *zia* Lina and cousin Maria had prepared a feast. They sat at the long harvest table that Ella's father had made, *zio* Domenicu told her, his eyes misting.

"He is with us in spirit today, along with your mother."

Ella's eyes misted, too, and when she dabbed at them, Angelica, who was seated beside her, gave her a hug. Ella returned Angelica's embrace, and when Ella straightened in her seat, she saw Massimo out of the corner of her eye reaching out to place his hand over hers. Confused by his caring gesture, after he had displayed indifference to her hug on Mount Tepilora, Ella slid her hand out from under his and avoided meeting Massimo's gaze, focusing instead on what her uncle was saying.

She bit her lip. There were so many emotions bouncing around in her chest right now, and she would need time to process them.

Zia Lina began passing around the serving dishes, joking in Italian *she* would start crying if they didn't eat before the food got cold. That lightened the atmosphere, and Ella laughed along with everyone. She praised her aunt and cousin for the amazing spread, starting with the platter of fried calamari, followed by baked eggplants and a tomato *ragù* of pork sausages served with *culurgiones*. For dessert, Maria brought out *pardulas*, small pies she had made filled with ricotta, saffron and lemon.

As Ella sipped her espresso, gazing at her relatives around the table, she felt that her heart was ready to burst with happiness. It was as if she had never left Sardinia, as if she'd had weekly dinners with her uncle, aunt and family, and this was one of those dinners.

It hadn't been awkward with Massimo, either, as she had initially feared. He had chatted easily with everyone in Italian and English and had even slipped into a lively Sardinian exchange with her uncle at one point. She had never seen Massimo smile or laugh so much, and every time her gaze returned to him, she had felt her pulse quickening.

Now *zio* Domenicu was saying that he was looking forward to getting to know Ella, and invited her again to stay at the farmhouse. "We have Maria's room empty," he said, before asking Ella where she had booked her accommodations.

She told them about the *agriturismo* and how she could visit often, once she rented a vehicle. As Ella described some of the features that had attracted her, she saw Maria and Tomasso exchange a surprised glance. And then they burst out laughing, joined in by her *zio* and *zia*. She cocked her head at them, puzzled by their reaction.

Her cousin gave her a beaming smile. "The *agriturismo* belongs to me and Tomasso," she said. "So now we know that the 'Ella Ross' who booked it is in fact our Marinella Rossi!"

By the time they arrived at Villa Serena, Massimo knew Ella was ready to call it a night. The meal and congenial conversation with her family had extended into late afternoon. Ella had been quiet during the car ride back and in the boat. He could see by her dreamy expression she was processing everything that had happened.

He was happy for her. Her relatives were good, hard-working people, and it had been obvious they were thrilled not only with Ella's return to Sardinia but with her intentions to spend time with them for a week. They had made it clear that she was welcome to visit whenever she could travel to Italy.

They had all been delighted to hear Ella had unknowingly booked the family *agriturismo*. And he had noted Ella and Maria, who he'd learned was six years younger than Ella, had really clicked. What a relief it must be for Ella to reconnect with her *zio* after all these years and know that he'd married and now had a family.

Along with the happiness he had felt for Ella during the visit, Massimo had also been aware of something stronger tugging at his chest. It had felt so right to be at Ella's side, not only witnessing but understanding her feelings. He had felt a powerful emotional connection that he had doubted he'd ever feel again with a woman. And he realized it was a connection that had begun the moment she had rammed into him at the airport and had grown steadily with each moment they had spent together.

When they came to the villa entrance, Massimo offered to walk her to the guesthouse.

"I'll be fine," she said, putting up a hand. "Thank you for driving me to Posada today. I hope you didn't mind the extended visit."

"Not at all. I enjoyed it." His eyes locked with Ella's. Her eyes were bright and her cheeks were flushed, the same color as the peonies in his gardens. Her lips, slightly open and free of lipstick, sparked a sizzle along his veins. Was he the only one feeling the magnetic pull, the aching desire to close the distance between them and…?

Massimo forced himself to look away. "I hope the good weather holds out for my mother's birthday tomorrow," he said, scanning the sky. "She deserves sunshine and blue skies... just like you," he added huskily.

"I hope so, too. *Buonasera*."

"Buonasera... Marinella."

Massimo watched her until she disappeared from view, and then he waited until he saw the lights of the guesthouse come on. He could hear his heart beating along with the swishing of the surf and the chirping of cicadas.

The afternoon with her newfound family had been so enjoyable. They had been so loving with Ella, and they had treated *him* like a member of the family, as well.

That's what he wanted, he realized.

To share Ella's family with her. But what did *she* want? Was there a chance in his wildest dreams that her feelings were the same?

Minutes later, soaking in his whirlpool tub and gazing at the gold-and-saffron bands around the setting sun and reflected in the calm sea waters, Massimo wondered how and when he could tell Marinella that he was ready...

For a second chance at love.

CHAPTER TWENTY-ONE

ELLA REACHED FOR her cell phone to stop the alarm. She had gone to bed too late last night. After returning to the guesthouse, she had been too wired to sleep. Thoughts of her family had swirled in her mind, along with a never ending loop of images of Massimo and twinges of regret that she had acted ungraciously when he had been trying to show her empathy.

After changing into a teddy, Ella had decided to transfer her mental energy to the piece she had started putting together for the magazine's August feature. The last interviews would take place at the *baronessa*'s birthday party and at the opening of the research center, but Ella had enough material to do a rough first draft.

Close to one-thirty in the morning, she had realized she had drifted off at the computer. She had turned it off and climbed into bed, exhausted but content with what she had accomplished. Once she had the rest of the material, she'd finish the piece in the next day or two, send it off, and then she'd have most of her holiday left. She couldn't wait to stay at Maria and Tomasso's *agriturismo* and spend more time with her family.

Ella forced herself to get out of bed. She strode to the balcony and looked out. *Baronessa* Silvia was going to get her blue skies and sunshine today. An unexpected lump formed in Ella's throat. She wished she could have spent more time with Massimo's mother. She would have loved to have had a cooking lesson with her.

And Massimo? her inner voice murmured.

Ella looked over the trees at *Villa Serena.* "Wishful thinking," she replied aloud. And then she berated herself for even entertaining such thoughts. Massimo DiLuca was out of reach. He had demonstrated that by the way he had frozen when she had hugged him. She had wanted to slink away in embarrassment...

But he hadn't been totally devoid of feelings. Extending his hand to her had been his attempt to show his empathy for her loss. He had lost his father. And his wife. He could identify with how Ella must have felt, learning that she was sitting at a table her father had made.

And then he had shown his warm side with

her family, chatting and laughing with each one of them. He had looked as if he were enjoying their company. Ella's heart had filled when she saw how he was with Angelica after lunch. She had brought out some toy figures, and he had played with her, assuming a different voice for each figure. Angelica had laughed each time and had given him a hug when he was done.

Ella had felt her heart twist. He would have made a great father, had he and his wife been able to adopt...

He could still be a father. If he allowed himself to date and eventually commit to a new relationship.

If he...

No! She needed to stop wasting her time in delusional thoughts. An espresso would help her clear her mind and focus on what she needed to do today. Without bothering to get dressed, she went downstairs, and a few minutes later, Ella had her espresso with one of the *pardulas* that Maria had made. Maria had run out of the farmhouse to hand Ella a container as she and Massimo were getting into his Lamborghini. "You can share them over breakfast," she had murmured in Italian, winking at Ella before running back inside.

Ella had immediately felt a hot tingling in

her cheeks. Massimo might not have seen Maria's sly wink, but he must have heard her words. For the entire drive, Ella had avoided looking at him, focusing instead on the passing scenery.

Now, biting into her second pastry, she thought about the birthday party that would be starting in a few hours. She would meet Massimo at his dock. It would be her last ride in his speedboat, and at the end of the party, he would be driving her to *Villa Paradiso*, where she would spend the night. And the following day, after the grand opening of the Cardiac Center, Maria and Tomasso would be picking her up and proceeding to their *agriturismo*.

Ella put down her cup and went to stand by the retractable glass door overlooking the cove. Opening it, she felt a wave of mingled awe and sadness as she took in the view. Awe at its timeless beauty and the perpetual motion of the sea. Sadness that she would be leaving this special haven the baron had chosen to help him heal. Her eyes welled up. How many times he must have stood here, too, witnessing the beauty of nature while feeling the ache of loss... It had been his retreat from the not so beautiful side of reality.

With a sigh, Ella climbed the spiral staircase to the loft. She surveyed the clothes still hanging in the closet. She might as well start packing, but first she needed to pick out what she wanted to wear to the *baronessa*'s party.

An hour later, Ella had her suitcase and carry-on luggage packed. She brought them down one at a time and set them by the entrance door. Returning to the loft, she glanced at the coral dress she had chosen and placed on the bed, a sleeveless maxi wrap dress with a tulip hem. She had bought it days before her flight to Sardinia, along with a red-coral bracelet and coral-flower studs.

After a last glance in the mirror and a quick scan of the room to make sure she had everything, Ella headed downstairs just as the doorbell rang. Her pulse leaped as she caught sight of Massimo at the glass door. Descending the spiral staircase, she took in his appearance in stages. Sunglasses. White shirt. Black trousers. Gleaming brown leather shoes. And back to his face.

His handsome face. A face she…*loved. The man she loved.*

Ella froze on the last step of the staircase. She stood immobilized. She had never allowed herself to admit this…until *now.* Now, on her last day on Massimo's island.

She had come to Sardinia with two intentions: to do the interviews for *Living the Life* magazine, and then to decide whether or not to connect with her uncle and his family if he had one. She had realized her first objectives.

And now she was ready to consider a third possibility...of returning and searching for her birth mother. Of course Ella had to also consider that if she located her mother, she might not want to connect with the daughter she had given up...for whatever reason. And Ella would feel the sting of being rejected a second time. Or she would be willing to establish some kind of relationship. Either scenario would be emotionally overwhelming.

She would work on preparing herself for either outcome.

It wouldn't happen during this trip. But Ella was determined to return to Sardinia again and again until the final piece of the puzzle of her history was found.

What about Massimo? her inner voice pressed.

Ella *hadn't* planned to fall for a Sardinian... To fall in love with a man whose heart had suffered, a heart she wanted to have and to hold...

Ella snapped out of her reverie. The only thing that she'd be holding soon was her luggage as Massimo dropped her off at *Villa Paradiso* after the party.

* * *

Massimo's breath caught in his throat as he watched Ella come down the spiral staircase. She looked…stunning. Like one of the coral roses in his gardens. His heart began a drumbeat that simultaneously excited and pained him.

He didn't want her to go back to Canada. He could handle her being with her Sardinian family for a week, but the painful part was accepting that she would be crossing the ocean soon and he might never see her again.

He couldn't let that happen.

The universe had taken someone away from him, and if that could happen, then the reverse could, too. He had to trust Rita was in another spiritual realm and she would want him to *live*, not hide himself away forever.

The universe was giving him another opportunity to love. And he wasn't going to blow it.

He had to tell—and show—Ella how he felt. That he wanted her, body and soul. That he wanted to share everything he had with her. And since she had reunited with her family, he'd do everything in his power to help her find her biological mother…if and when she was ready.

She opened the door and he stepped inside. *"Sei bellissima, Marinella."*

"Grazie." She frowned, almost as if she couldn't believe he was saying such a thing. She leaned over to pick up her briefcase and the small carry-on.

"I—I have to tell you something," he said gruffly. "I should have told you yesterday…"

She set down the items and looked up at him.

"I don't want you to go."

Ella's brows furrowed. "Your mother's expecting me."

He laughed softly. "Not *there*, silly."

She shook her head. "I don't understand."

"I don't want you to leave Sardinia."

"You're joking."

"No, non scherzo, Marinella."

"Uh, w-why? I mean, why not?" Ella blinked.

"Because I have fallen with my head over my heels for you." He looked at her tenderly, hoping she would see that his words—whether he had gotten them right or wrong—were spoken with his heart.

"But…yesterday you acted as if I was poison when I hugged you."

"I wasn't expecting a hug. And you moved away too quickly, as if *I* was poison." He gently cupped her chin with one hand and bent his head to look deeply into her eyes. "I want you to be in my life, Marinella. Not just for this week but for always. *Per eternità.*"

She shook her head. "Someone pinch me," she murmured. "I must be dreaming."

Massimo gave a soft laugh. "I'm not going to pinch you. I never want to hurt you. And no, you are not dreaming." He leaned closer and kissed her coral lips. "I have so much I want to tell you," he murmured against her ear. "But I need to know something…"

"Yes."

"Do you…" He kissed her again, thoroughly.

"I said yes," she said, breathless.

"But you don't know what I'm about to ask…" He stroked her temple before tracing her lips with his fingers.

"I do."

"You can read my mind, *bella*?" His arms encircled her waist and he pulled her close.

She pressed her cheek against his chest. "I can read *this*," she said, tapping his heart with her finger. "And it's going faster than your Lamborghini Huracán."

Massimo chuckled softly and took her left hand in his. "Marinella, you brought laughter and happiness back into my life. I said I don't want you to leave Sardinia, but I can accept you traveling back to Canada when you want to. With *me*. I have yet to explore that magnificent country." He paused for a moment, conscious of the pounding in his chest.

"I don't want to hide from life anymore, Marinella." He rubbed along his chin. "See? That's why I shaved most of my beard off. I'm ready to show my face again. To live again. With *you*, my Sardinian beauty." He embraced her tightly, kissing her forehead. "*Ti amo, Marinella.* And I would be the happiest man in the world if you would accompany me to my mother's birthday and the opening of the Research Center tomorrow, *amore mio*. And be with me for the rest of my life... *Va bene?*" His lips brushed gentle kisses over her temple, cheek and ended with a hungry kiss that left them both breathless.

"*Va bellissimo,*" she replied with a sigh. She looked up to gaze lovingly into his dark eyes before flashing him a mischievous grin. "Now can we get going? I'm dying to taste your mother's food."

He laughed and pointed to her luggage. "How about we leave this at my—*our*—villa? We can sleep in tomorrow morning and enjoy Maria's *pardulas* for breakfast." He winked before scooping Ella up in his arms and twirling her around, his heart bursting as she wrapped her arms tightly around his neck and murmured, "*Ti amo, Massimo...*" in his ear.

EPILOGUE

ELLA BLINKED AS the sunlight caught on her vintage solitaire engagement ring, the two-carat stone absolutely stunning in an intricate floral setting and filigreed band. And next to it, her gold wedding band in its elegant simplicity. She never tired of looking at them, just like she never tired of looking at her husband.

Now she knew what her dear mother had meant about a man putting stars in her eyes...

From the moment Massimo had uttered *"Ti amo"* before his mother's birthday celebration, Ella's heart had overflowed with the love that had been developing since she set foot on his island. Her island, too.

Sardinia belonged to both of them. And they would continue to live at *Villa Serena*. See the glorious sun rise and set together.

She would enjoy learning how to prepare traditional Sardinian dishes with the *baronessa*, who had embraced her with tears in her eyes when Ella and Massimo had told her that they would be getting married and spending the rest of their lives together. They had waited until all her birthday guests had left and were enjoying a celebratory drink of *mirto* in her gardens when Massimo had shared the news. Silvia's eyes had widened as she glanced from Massimo to Ella, and then she had leaped up, and with clasped hands and eyes directed skyward, she thanked the heavens and declared that they had just given her the best birthday gift of all.

A few days later, Chef Angelo had brought over a vintage bottle of champagne and had prepared a special dinner in their honor…a new dish he'd named *Il Mare per Marinella*— The Sea for Marinella—a lobster bisque and sautéed scallops drizzled with Sardinian lemons and Canadian maple syrup.

Ella had attended the official opening of the DiLuca Cardiac Research Center with her uncle Domenicu and his family. She and Massimo had decided that they would wait to make a public announcement about their engagement, to keep the focus on the Center.

Ella had watched Massimo, standing tall and gorgeous at the black-tie event, as he shared what the Cardiac Research Center meant for him and his mother. His voice had wavered slightly as he announced that it was their gift to the community and the world in honor of his late wife and father. And the *baronessa* had spoken next, graciously thanking everyone who had had a hand in the development of the Center, and declaring her and Massimo's confidence and best wishes for the renowned team of researchers whose work the DiLucas were proud to support.

Everyone had fallen silent, and the room had erupted in applause while photographers and a television crew hovered around Massimo and his mother, visibly excited about the baron's reappearance in public.

Ella had worn an elegant black gown with satin accents and a silver shawl. As the cameras had flashed around him, he had looked toward the crowd and his gaze had connected with hers. His serious expression had given way to a smile, one that Ella knew without a doubt was meant for her, and her alone.

And then he and the *baronessa* had cut the ribbon, followed by the celebratory banquet. Although Massimo and Silvia were seated at the head table with local dignitaries and the leader of the research team, they both went around after the dinner to mingle and thank the guests at each table.

Ella had felt a rush of heat searing through

her veins at the way Massimo's eyes had swept over her before meeting hers. And she had experienced the same feeling later at *Villa Serena*, when they were standing on his balcony. The indigo sky looked like a velvet dress sparkling with sequins, making Ella feel like she was in an enchanted world.

Massimo had gently removed her shawl and after looking deeply into her eyes, had bent to trace the length of her neck with soft kisses. Each one had sent her pulse racing, and by the time his lips had reached hers, Ella's heart was pounding. She had wrapped her arms around his neck and returned his kiss with a hunger that matched his.

And when she had thought she'd ignite from the passion between them, Massimo had swooped her up and carried her to his bed.

He had shown his love for her with his body and soul all night, the starlight from the open doors of the balcony mesmerizing on the curves of their bodies. Ella had lost herself in the stars Massimo had put in her eyes, and they both lost track of the times they had murmured *"Ti amo"* to each other.

Ella had thought her heart would burst from happiness and joy.

She had spent the following day finishing her piece for *Living the Life*, and emailed it to her boss, satisfied and excited. An hour later, Paul had called her to congratulate her, impressed and enthused, as well. Ella had stunned him with the news about her and Massimo after that and promised to call him with the details after her holiday.

The week in Posada had been delightful. She had spent the days getting to know her *zio* Domenicu and his family, who had showered her with love and affection. And had included her in their farm and *agriturismo* routines. During quiet moments alone with her uncle, he had revealed a few details his brother Micheli had shared with him secretly about something he alone had known about Ella's young birth mother. He had discovered this information after accidentally overhearing part of a conversation at the adoption agency before a scheduled meeting...

Ella had felt a shift in her heart at the news. She had felt both anxious and excited. When she had told Massimo later, he'd promised to contact people who would investigate the proper social-services channels to possibly locate her.

During her week in Posada, Massimo had insisted that she enjoy this time without him, although he had always traveled back from *Villa Serena* to join them for a fabulous dinner.

And to join Ella later in her bed...

She smiled now, watching him approach with a breakfast tray. It was a glorious day in early September, warm and sunny, and she had wanted to sit out on the living room patio. They were still in their robes and had planned to spend the day relaxing and going over their plans for a five-day visit to the Maddalena Islands. They would be presiding at the official opening of their new DiLuca resort and staying in the penthouse suite reserved exclusively for them.

Massimo's eyes had twinkled like the diamond ring he'd held when he had proposed to Ella on his yacht during a weekend trip to check out the new resort back in August. After sliding the ring on her finger and giving her a kiss that was as scorching as the Sardinian sun, he had told her he had decided to call the resort *Il Mare di Marinella*—Marinella's Sea.

She had been moved to tears and declared that she would come up with a surprise for him.

Two weeks later, they had exchanged vows in a private church ceremony near the *baronessa*'s villa, followed by a small reception for their closest friends in her gardens. The wedding planners had decorated the tent canopy and tables with flowers that Silvia had wanted Ella and Massimo to choose from her own gardens, and Chef Angelo had picked a special team to prepare a sumptuous seven-course dinner. Ella had insisted on spending their wedding night at *Villa Serena*, where their love had begun.

The rest of August had passed with every moment spent together there, creating new memories…

And now, she was ready to give Massimo the surprise she had promised him.

His hair still tousled, he smiled crookedly as he placed the tray down and leaned over to kiss her. "I want to spend the rest of my life like this, Marinella, enjoying the peace and quiet of our island together."

He poured the espresso and set it down before sitting across from her.

She shook her head. "It won't be quiet for long, *amore*." She smiled and arched her eyebrows.

His brow furrowed and he set down the cup with a clatter. And then his eyes widened. "Do you mean…? *Are you…are we—?*"

"Yes! I am, *amore*! We're going to have a ba—"

He leaped up and kissed her, cradling the back of her head. When he pulled back, he put a tentative hand on Ella's belly, his eyes misting.

"I told you I'd come up with a surprise for you…" Her voice wavered, and she tried to blink back her own tears, but they started trickling down her cheeks.

"You made me the happiest man in the world when you told me you loved me and would be my wife," he murmured, wiping her cheeks with the sash of her robe. "And now, you've given me the best gift I could ever hope for." He looked deeply into her eyes. "Do you know when…?"

"The night of the official opening of the Center. Remember the sky that night? I had never seen so many stars in the heavens."

"And I was in heaven that night, seeing the stars in your eyes," he said huskily, kissing her again.

Ella sighed contentedly. "Well, what do you think about naming our baby Stellina…our little star? I just have this feeling we're going to have a girl."

He gazed at her thoughtfully for a moment. "Do you know what a 'blue star' is?"

Ella frowned. "No. I've never heard the term. Why?"

"In astrological terms, a blue star has a mass greater than the sun, and is one of the brightest in the constellation, appearing blue to the human eye."

Ella cocked her head at him, wondering where he was going with this.

"And so, Marinella, why don't we call our baby Stellina Celeste? Our little blue star?"

"It's perfect," she murmured, wrapping her arms around his neck and kissing him.

"And if we have a boy?" His brow furrowed. "We should have a name in mind, just in case."

"How about Angelo? Our little angel?"

Massimo let out a deep laugh. "I know someone who would be absolutely thrilled. Either way, Chef Angelo can be the baby's godfather."

He waved a hand at the breakfast tray. "Now I get why you haven't been wanting your usual espresso... How about one of these *sebadas*? You need to keep up your strength, *amore*. Are you hungry?"

Ella cupped his chin and turned his face her way. "*Sì, barone.* Very." She grinned, and showed him with her kiss.

* * * * *

If you enjoyed this story,
check out these other great reads from
Rosanna Battigelli

Rescued by the Guarded Tycoon
Caribbean Escape with the Tycoon
Captivated by Her Italian Boss
Swept Away by the Enigmatic Tycoon

All available now!